FULL CYCLE

By
CLIFFORD D. SIMAK

ARMCHAIR FICTION
PO Box 4369, Medford, Oregon   97501-0168

*For more information about Armchair Books and products, visit our
website at...*

www.armchairfiction.com

Or email us at...

armchairfiction@yahoo.com

A STRANGE NEW WORLD OF THE FUTURE!

Was Ambrose Wilson merely a ghost…an ancient relic of a new world that had passed him by? Was there no place in this neo-culture for a man who had made history his life? Surely, somewhere, there must be a link between yesterday and the tomorrow that had already arrived…

However, it took great hardship and the worst kind of personal betrayal to help him realize mankind's new, untapped potential in this thought-provoking tale of the future, by one of science fiction's very best writers, Clifford D. Simak.

FOR A COMPLETE SECOND NOVEL, TURN TO PAGE 73

CAST OF CHARACTERS

DR. AMBROSE WILSON
He was an anachronism in a new world that he refused to take part in—until fate cast him on the road to a new civilization.

JAKE
He was Doc's best friend—loyal to the end. But then the world threw things in his path that made him reconsider…

THE STUFFY
Just like an old-style English squire. He lived in a big house and owned a big factory—until his men all walked out on him.

THE OLD MAN
A friendly old cuss from a farming camp. He knew his camp's rainmakers could open up the skies—without cloud seeding!

FRED
Like so many other camp business agents, he was open and friendly, but hesitant about taking on newcomers.

RAY, THE TRUCKER
Like so many others in the new world, he failed to realize the unique powers and possibilities that lay within man's grasp.

TOM
He had been a professor at a big university. Now, however, he used his brain in ways he had never thought possible.

CHAPTER ONE

THE LETTER sent the life of Amby Wilson crashing decorously down about his ears. It was a form affair, with the address typed in with a newer, blacker ribbon; it said:

Dr. Ambrose Wilson,
Department of History
 It is with regret that I must inform you the board of regents at their meeting this morning decided the university will cease to function at the end of the present term.
 Contributing to the decision were the lack of funds and the progressive dwindling of the student body. You, of course, have been aware of the situation for some time, but nevertheless...

There was more of it, but Amby didn't read it. What still was left unread, he knew, would be no more than the grossest of platitudes.

It had been bound to happen.

The regents had hung on in the face of monstrous difficulties; the university was virtually deserted. The place that once had rung with life and pulsed with learning was now no better than a ghost school.

As the city was a ghost city.

And I a ghost; thought Amby.

He made an admission to himself, an admission he would not have made a day or hour ago: For thirty years or more he had lived in an unreal and unsubstantial world, clinging to the old, vague way of life as he first had known it. And to make that vague life the more substantial, he had banished to an intellectual outer limbo any valid consideration of the world beyond the city.

And good reason that he should, he thought; good and valid reason. What was outside the city had no link with this world of his. A nomad population—an almost alien people, who had built a neo-culture rich in decadence, concocted half of provincialism, half of old folk-tales.

There was nothing there, he thought, of any value to a man like him, nothing worth the consideration of a man like him. Here in this university he had kept alight a feeble glow of the old learning and the old tradition; now the light had flickered out and the learning and tradition would go down into the darkness.

And that, he knew, was no attitude for a historian to take; history was the truth and the seeking after truth. To gloss over, to ignore, to push away an eventful fact—no matter how distasteful was not the way of history.

Now history had caught up with him and there were two alternatives. He could go out and face the world or he could hide from it. There was no compromise.

Amby picked up the letter between his fingertips, as if it might be something dead and left out in the sun too long. Carefully he dropped it in the wastebasket; then he got his old felt hat and clapped it on his head.

He marched out of the classroom without looking back.

CHAPTER TWO

WHEN HE got home, a scarecrow was perched on the front steps. When it saw him coming, it pulled itself together and got up. "Evening, Doc," it said.

"Good evening, Jake," said Amby.

"I was just fixing to go fishing," Jake told him.

Amby sat down carefully on the steps and shook his head. "Not tonight; don't feel up to it. They're closing down the university."

Jake sat down beside him and stared across the street at the city wilderness. "I suppose that ain't no big surprise to you."

"I've been expecting it," said Amby. "Nobody attends any more except some *stuffy* kids. All the *nomies* go to their own universities, if that is what they call them. Although to tell you the honest truth, Jake, I can't see how schools like those could give them very much."

"Well, you're fixed all right, I guess," said Jake, consolingly. "You been working all these years; you probably been able to put away a little. Now with me it's different. We been living hand-to-mouth and we always will."

"I'm not too well fixed," said Amby, "but I'll get along somehow. I probably haven't too long left; I'm almost seventy."

"There was a day," said Jake, "when they had a law that paid a man to quit at sixty five. But the *nomies* threw that out, just like they did everything."

He picked up a short length of dead branch and dug

absentmindedly at the grass. "I always figured, someday I'd get me enough together so I could buy a trailer. You can't do a thing unless you got a trailer. It does beat all how times can change. I remember when I was a kid it was the man who owned a house that was all set for life. But now a house don't count for nothing. You got to have a trailer."

He got up in sections, stood with his rags fluttering in the wind, looking down at Amby. "You ain't changed your mind about that fishing, Doc?"

"I'm all beat out," said Amby.

"With you not working any more," Jake said, "us two can get in a powerful lot of hunting. The place is full of squirrels and the young rabbits will soon be big enough to eat. This fall there'll be a sight of coons. Now that you ain't working, I'll split the skins with you."

"You still can keep the skins," said Amby.

Jake stuck his thumbs into his waistband and spat upon the ground. "Might just as well spend your time out in the woods as anywhere. Used to be a man could make some money if he was lucky at his prowling, but prowling now is just a waste of time. The places all have been worked over and it's getting so it's downright dangerous to go inside of them. You never know when something might give way and come down and hit you or when the floor will drop out from underneath you."

He hitched up his britches. "Remember that time we found the box with all the jewelry in it?"

Amby nodded. "I remember that; you almost got enough to buy the trailer that time."

"Ain't it a fact? It does beat all how a man can fritter cash away. I bought a new gun and a batch of cartridges and some clothes for the family—and lord knows, we needed them—and a good supply of grub; and before I knew it there wasn't near enough left over to even think about a trailer. In the old days a man could have bought one on time. All he'd needed would be ten percent to pay down on it. But you can't do that no more. There aren't even any banks. And no loan companies. Remember, Doc, when the place crawled with loan companies?"

"It all has changed," said Amby. "When I think back it can't seem possible."

But it was, of course.

The city was gone as an institution; the farms had become corporations and people no longer lived in houses—only the *stuffies* and the squatters.

And folks like me, thought Amby.

CHAPTER THREE

IT WAS a crazy idea—sign of old age and feeble-mindedness, perhaps. A man of sixty-eight, a man of competence and settled habits, did not go charging off on a wild adventure even if his world had crashed about his ears.

He tried to quit thinking of it, but he couldn't quit. He thought about it all the time that he cooked supper, and while he ate supper, and later when he washed the dishes.

With the dishes done, he went into the living room, carrying the kitchen lamp. He set the lamp on a table beside another lamp and lit the second lamp. *Must be a sign a man's eyes are wearing out,* he thought, *when he needs two lamps to read by.* But kerosene lamps, at best, were poor things; not like electricity.

He picked a book out of the shelves and settled down to read, but he couldn't read; he couldn't keep his mind on what he tried to read. He finally gave it up.

He took one of the lamps, walked to the fireplace and held it high so that the lamplight fell upon the painting there. And he wondered as he raised the lamp if she would smile at him tonight; he was fairly sure she would, for she was always ready with a tiny smile when he needed it the most.

He wasn't sure at first if she were smiling; then he saw she was, and he stood there looking at her and her smile.

There had been many times of late when he talked with her, for he remembered how ready she had always been to listen to him, how he had talked out his troubles and his triumphs—although, come to think of it, his triumphs had been few.

But he could not talk to her tonight; she would not understand. This world in which he lived without her would seem to her so topsy-turvy as to be past all understanding. And if he tried to talk to her about it, she would be disturbed and troubled and he must not let that happen.

You'd think, he told himself, upbraiding himself, that I'd be content to leave well enough alone. I have a place to hide. I could live out my life in comfort and in safety. And that, he knew, was the way he wanted it to be.

But there was that nagging voice that talked inside his brain: *You have failed your task and failed it willingly. You have shut your eyes and failed. You have failed by looking backwards. The true historian does not live in the past alone. He must use the past to understand the present; and he must know them both if he is to see the trend toward the future.*

But I do not want to know the future, said the stubborn Dr. Ambrose Wilson.

And the nagging voice said: *The future is the only thing that is worth the knowing.*

HE STOOD silently, holding the lamp above his head, staring at the painting almost as if he expected it to speak, as if it might give a sign.

There wasn't any sign. There couldn't be a sign, he knew. It was no more than a painting of a woman, dead these thirty years. The sensed nearness, the old sharp memory, the smile upon the lips were in the heart and mind—not in the square of canvas with clever brush strokes that preserved across the years the bright illusion of a loved face.

He lowered the lamp and went back to his chair.

There was so much to say, he thought, and no one to say it to—although the house might listen if he talked to it as an ancient friend. It had been a friend, he thought. It had been lonely often with her no longer here—but not as lonely in the house as away from it, for the house was a part of her.

He was safe here, safe in this anachronistic house, safe in the abandoned city with its empty buildings; comfortable in this city gone back to wilderness, filled with squirrels and rabbits, colorful and fragrant now with the bloom of gone-wild lilacs and escaped daffodils, prowled by squatters who hunted the thickets of its lawns for game and prowled its crumbling structures to find some salvage they might sell.

Queer, he thought, the concepts upon which a culture might be founded, the fantastic acceptance standards that evolved in each society.

Some forty years ago, the cleavage of the culture had first started; it had not come all at once, but quickly enough so that historically it must be regarded as an abrupt rather than a gradual cleavage.

It had been the Year of Crisis, he remembered, when the drums of fear had thudded through the land and a man had lain in bed, tensed and listening for the coming of the bomb, knowing even as he listened that he'd not hear it if it came.

Fear was the start of it, he thought; and what and where would be the end?

He sat huddled in his chair, cringing from the dark barbarism that lay beyond the city—an old man caught between the future and the past.

CHAPTER FOUR

JAKE SAID, "She's a beauty, Doc." He got up to walk around it once again.

"Yes, sir," he said, patting it. "She surely is a beauty. I don't think I can rightly say I ever saw a finer trailer. And I've seen lots of them."

"We may be doing a lot of traveling in it," Amby told him. "We want one that will stand up. The roads, I understand, aren't what they used to be. The *nomies* chisel on the road tax, and the government hasn't got much money to keep the roads in shape."

"It won't take long," Jake said confidently. "All we got to do is just kind of look around. In no time at all we'll find a camp that will take us in. Stands to reason there'll be one of them that could find a use for us."

He went over to the trailer and carefully wiped a spot of dust off its shiny surface with his ragged shirtsleeve.

"We ain't none of us scarcely slept a wink since you told us, Doc. Myrt, she can't understand it; she keeps saying to me, 'Why is Doc taking us along? We ain't got no claim on him; all we been is neighbors.' "

"I'm a bit too old," said Amby, "to do it by myself. I have to have someone along to help out with the driving and the other chores. And you've been looking forward all these years to going trailering."

"That's a fact," admitted Jake. "Doc, you never spoke a truer word. I wanted it so bad I could almost taste it; and by the looks of it, so have all the rest of us. You ought to see the throwing away and packing that's going on over at the house. Myrt is plain beside herself. I tell you, Doc, it ain't no safe place to go until Myrt calms down a bit."

"Maybe I ought to do some packing myself," said Amby. "Not that there's much to do; I'll just leave the most of it behind."

But he didn't stir. He didn't want to face it.

It would be hard to leave his home—although that was old-fogey thinking, for there were no longer any homes. "Home" was a word out of an era left behind. "Home" was another nostalgic word for old men like him to mumble in their dim remembering. "Home" was the symbol of a static culture that had failed in the scales of Man's survival. To put down roots, to stay and become encumbered by possessions—not only physical, but mental and traditional as well—was to die. To be mobile and forever poised on the edge of flight, to travel lean and gaunt, to shun encumbrances, was the price of freedom and life.

Full cycle, Amby thought—*we have come full cycle. From tribe to city, now back to tribe again.*

Jake came back from the trailer and sat down again. "Tell me, Doc; tell me honest now—why are you doing it? Not that I ain't glad you are, for otherwise I'd never in all my born days get out of this here rat trap. But I can't somehow get it through my head why you are pulling stakes. You ain't a young man, Doc, and…"

"I know," said Amby; "maybe that's the reason. Not too much time left, and I have to make the best use of it I can."

"You're sitting pretty, Doc, and not a worry in the world. Now that you've retired, you could take it easy and have a lot of fun."

"I've got to find out," said Amby.

"Find out what?"

"I don't know; just what is happening, I guess."

They sat quietly, looking at the trailer in all its shining glory. From some distance down the street came the faint clatter of pots and pans and a suddenly raised voice.

Myrt still was busy packing.

CHAPTER FIVE

THE FIRST evening they stopped at a deserted campsite across the road from an idle factory.

It was an extensive camp and it had the look of being occupied only recently, as if the trailers might have pulled out just a day or two before. There were fresh tire tracks in the dust; scraps of paper still blew about the area, and the ground beneath some of the water faucets still was damp.

Jake and Amby sat in the trailer's shade and looked at the silent buildings just across the road.

"Funny thing," said Jake, "about this place not running. Sign up there says it's a food processing plant. Breakfast food, looks like. Figure maybe it shut down because there wasn't any market for the stuff it makes?"

"That might be it," said Amby. "But seems there should be a market for breakfast cereal, at least some sort of market for it. Enough to keep it running, although maybe not at full capacity."

"Figure there was some kind of trouble?"

"No sign of it," said Amby.

"Looks as if they just up and left."

"There's that big house up on the hill. Look, up that-away…"

"I see it now," said Amby. "Might be where the *stuffy* lives."

"Could be."

"Wonder what it would be like to be a *stuffy*? Just sit and watch the cash come rolling in. Let other people work for you. Have everything you want. Never want for nothing."

"I imagine," Amby told him, "that the *stuffies* have their troubles, too."

"I'd like to have them kind of troubles. I'd just plumb love to have them kind of troubles for a year or two."

He spat on the ground and hauled himself erect. "Might go out and see if I could get me a rabbit or a squirrel," he said. "You feel like coming with me?"

Amby shook his head. "I'm a little tuckered out."

"Probably won't find nothing anyhow. Close to a camp like this, the game must be all cleaned out."

"After a while," said Amby, "when I'm rested up a bit, I might take a walk."

CHAPTER SIX

THE HOUSE was a *stuffy* house, all right. One could almost smell the money of it. It was large and sprawling, very neatly kept, and surrounded by extensive grounds full of flowers and shrubs.

Amby sat down on a stone wall just outside the grounds and looked back the way he'd come. There below him lay the factory and the deserted camping grounds, with his trailer standing alone in the great level, trampled area. The road wound away to a far horizon, white in the summer sun, and there was nothing on it—not a single car or truck or trailer. And that, he thought, was not the way it had been. Once the roads had been crawling with machines.

But this was a different world than the one he'd known. It was a world that he'd ignored for more than thirty years, and it had grown alien in those thirty years. He had shut himself away from it and lost it; now that he sought it once again, he found it puzzling and at times a little terrifying.

A voice spoke behind him. "Good evening, sir."

Amby turned and saw the man—middle-aged or more, and the tweeds and pipe. Almost, he thought, like the age-old tradition of the English country squire.

"Good evening," Amby said. "I hope I'm not intruding."

"Not at all. I saw you camped down there; very glad to have you."

"My partner went out hunting, so I took a walk."

"You folks changing?"

"Changing?"

"Changing camps, I mean. There used to be a lot of it. Not much any more."

"You mean changing from one camp to another?"

"That's it. A process of settling down, I take it. Get dissatisfied with one setup, so go out and hunt another."

"By now," said Amby, "the shakedown period must be almost over. By now each man must have found his place."

The *stuffy* nodded. "Maybe that's the way it is. I don't know too much about it."

"Nor I," Amby told him.

"We're just starting out. My university closed down, so I bought a trailer. My next door neighbors came along with me. This is our first day."

"I've often thought," said the man, "that it might be fun to do a little touring. When I was a boy we used to go on long motoring trips and visit different places; but there doesn't seem to be much of that any more. Used to be places where you could stop the night—motels, they called them. And every mile or so there were eating places and service stations where you could buy gasoline. Now the only place where you can get anything to eat, or buy some gas, is at one of the camps; lots of times, I understand, they don't care to sell."

"But we aren't touring. We hope to join a camp."

The *stuffy* stared at him for a moment, then he said: "I wouldn't have thought so, looking at you."

"You don't approve of it?"

"Don't mind me," the *stuffy* said. "Right at this moment, I'm a little sour on them. Just the other morning they all drove out on me. Closed down the plant. Left me sitting here."

He climbed up on the wall and sat down alongside Amby. "They wanted to take me over completely, you understand," he said, settling down to a minute recounting of it. "Under the existing contract they already ran the plant. They bought the raw materials and set up their own work schedules and kept up maintenance. They decided plant operation policy and set production schedules. I'd have had to ask their permission just to go down there and visit. But it wasn't enough for them. Do, you know what they wanted?"

Amby shook his head.

"They wanted to take over marketing. That was all that I had left and they wanted to take that away from me. They were all set to shove me out completely. Pay me a percentage of the profit and cut me out entirely."

"Somehow," Amby said, "that doesn't sound quite fair."

"And when I refused to sign, they just packed up and left."

"A strike?"

"I suppose you could call it that. A most effective one."

"What do you do now?"

"Wait until another camp comes down the road. There'll be one along sometime. They'll see the plant standing idle, and if they're industrial and think they can handle it, they'll come up and see me. Maybe we can make a deal. Even if we can't, there'll be another camp along. There's always floating camps. Either that or swarms."

"Swarms?"

"Like bees, you know. A camp gets overcrowded. Too many to handle the contract that they have. So it up and swarms. Usually a bunch of young folks just starting out in life. A swarm is usually easier to deal with than the floaters. The floaters, often as not are a bunch of radicals and malcontents who, can't get along with anyone, while the youngsters in a swarm are anxious to get started at something of their own."

"That all sounds swell enough," said Amby, "but how about the ones who left you? Could they afford just to pull stakes and go?"

"They're loaded," said the *stuffy*. "They worked here almost twenty years. They got a sinking fund that would choke a cow."

"I didn't know," said Amby.

There was so much, he thought, that he didn't know. Not only the thinking and the customs, but even a lot of the terminology was strange.

IT HAD BEEN different in the old days when there'd been a daily press; when a new phrase or a new thought became public property almost overnight; when the forces that shaped one's life were daily spread before one in the black and white of print. But now there were no papers and no television. There still was radio of course; but radio, he thought, was a poor medium to keep a man in touch; even so, it was not the kind of radio he'd known and he never listened to it.

There were no papers and no television, and that wasn't all by any means. There was no furniture, for there was no need of furniture in a trailer with everything built in. There were no rugs, no carpeting, no drapes. There were few luxury items, for there was no room for luxury items in the confines of a trailer. There were no formal and no party clothes, for no one in a trailer camp would dress—there was no room for an extensive wardrobe and the close communal life would discourage all formality. Such dress as there might be in a trailer camp undoubtedly would run heavily to sports-wear.

There were no banks or insurance firms or loan companies. Social security had gone down the drain. There was no use for banks or loan companies; the credit union setup, dating from the old trade unionism, would have replaced them on a tight communal basis. And an extension of the old union health and welfare fund, once again on a tight communal basis, had replaced any need of social security, governmental welfare aid, or health insurance. And the war chest idea—once again grafted from unionism—had made each trailer camp an independent, self-sufficient governmental unit.

It worked all right, for there was little that a resident of a trailer camp could spend his money on. The old flytraps of entertainment; the need of expensive dress; the overhead of house furnishings—all had been wiped out. Thrift had become an enforced virtue—enforced by circumstance.

A man didn't even pay taxes any more—not to speak of, anyhow. State and local governments long ago had fallen by the wayside. There remained nothing but the federal government, and even the federal government had lost much of its control—as it must have known it would on that day of forty years ago. All that need now be paid was a trifling defense tax, and a slightly heavier road tax, and the *nomies* screamed loud and lustily against the paying of the road tax.

"It's not like it used to be," said the *stuffy*. "This trade unionism got entirely out of hand."

"It was about all the people had to tie to," Amby told him. "It was the one surviving piece of logic, the one remaining solid thing that was left to them. Naturally, they embraced it; it took the place of government."

"The government should have done it differently," said the *stuffy*.

"They might have if we hadn't got so frightened. It was the fear that did it; it would have been all right if we hadn't got afraid."

Said the *stuffy*: "We'd been blown plumb to hell if we hadn't got afraid."

"Maybe so," said Amby. "I can remember how it happened. The order went out to decentralize, and I guess industry must have known a good deal more about what the situation was then the most of us; it got out and scattered, without any argument. Maybe they knew the government wasn't fooling and maybe they had some facts that weren't public knowledge. Although the public facts, as I remember them, ran rather to the grim side."

"I was just in my teens then," said the *stuffy*, "but I remember something of it. Real estate worth nothing. Couldn't sell city property at a fraction of its worth. And the workers couldn't stay there, for their jobs had moved away— away out in the country. Decentralization took in a lot of country. The big plants split up, some of them into a lot of smaller units and there had to be a lot of miles between each unit."

Amby nodded. "So there'd be no target big enough for anyone to waste a bomb on. Make it cost too much to wipe out an industry. Where one bomb would have done the job before, now it would take a hundred."

"I don't know," said the *stuffy*, still unwilling to concede. "Seems to me the government could have handled it a little differently instead of letting the thing run on the way it did."

"I suspect the government had a lot on its mind right then."

"Sure it had, but it had been in the housing business up to its ears before. Building all sorts of low-cost housing projects."

"It had the job of helping industry get those new plants set up. And the trailers solved the housing problem for the moment."

"I suppose," the *stuffy* said, "that was the way it was."

And that, of course, was the way it had been.

THE WORKERS had been forced to follow their jobs— either follow them or starve. Unable to sell their houses in the cities when the bottom dropped out of the real estate market almost overnight, they compromised on trailers; and around each fractionated industry grew up a trailer camp.

They grew to like the trailer life, perhaps, or they were afraid to build another house for fear the same thing might happen yet again—even if some could afford to build another house, and there were a lot of them who couldn't. Or they may have become disillusioned and disgusted—it did not matter what. But the trailer life had caught on and stayed, and people who were not directly affected by decentralization had gradually drifted into the trailer camps, until even most of the villages stood empty.

The cult of possessions had been foresworn. The tribe sprang up again.

Fear had played its part and freedom—the freedom from possessions, and the freedom to pick up and go without ever looking back and unionism, too.

For the trailer movement had killed the huge trade union setup. Union bosses and business agents, who had found it easy to control one huge union setup found it a sheer impossibility to control the hundred scattered units into which each big local had been broken. But within each trailer camp a local brand of unionism had caught on with renewed force and significance. It had served to weld each camp into a solid and cohesive unit. It had made the union a thing close to each family's heart and interest. Unionism, interpreted in the terms of the people and their needs, had provided the tribal pattern needed to make the trailer system work.

"I'll say this much for them," the *stuffy* said. "They were an efficient bunch. They ran the plant better than I could have run it; they watched the costs and they were forever digging up shortcuts and improvements. During the twenty years they worked here they practically redesigned that plant. That's one of the things they pointed out to me in negotiations. But I told them they'd done it to protect their jobs, and that may have been the thing that made them sore enough to leave."

He tapped his pipe out on the wall. "You know," he said, "I'm not too sure but what I'm right. It'll more than likely take any new gang that moves in a month or so to figure out all the jackleg contraptions that this bunch of mine rigged up. All I hope is that they don't start it up too quick and wreck the whole shebang."

He polished the bowl of his pipe abstractedly. "I don't know. I wish I could figure that tribe out—just for my peace of mind, if nothing else. They were good people and mostly sensible. They were hard workers and up to a month ago easy to get along with. They lived normal lives for the most part, but there were things about them I couldn't understand. Like the superstitions that grew up. They'd worked up a sizeable list of taboos, and they were hell on signs of exorcism and placation. Oh, sure, I know we use to do it— cross your fingers and spit over your left shoulder and all that sort of stuff—but with us it was all in fun. It was just horseplay with us. A sort of loving link with a past we were reluctant to give up. But these people, I swear, believed and lived by it."

"That," said Amby, "bears out my own belief that the culture has actually degenerated into the equivalent of tribalism, perhaps further than I thought. Your small, compact, enclosed social groups give rise to that sort of thing. In a more integrated culture, such notions are laughed out of existence; but in protected soil they take root and grow."

"The farm camps are the worst," the *stuffy* told him. "They have rainmaking mumbo-jumbo and crop magic and all the rest of it."

Amby nodded. "That makes sense. There's something about the enigma of the soil and seed that encourages mysticism. Remember the wealth of mythology that grew up around agriculture in prehistoric times—the fertility rites, and the lunar planting tables, and all the other fetishes."

He sat on the stone wall, staring off across the land; out of the dark unknown of the beginning of the race, he seemed to hear the stamp of callused feet, the ritual chant, the scream of the sacrifice.

CHAPTER SEVEN

THE NEXT DAY, from the top of a high hill, they sighted the farm camp. It was located at the edge of a grove of trees a little distance from a row of elevators, and across the plains that stretched in all directions lay the gold-green fields.

"Now that's the kind of place I'd like to settle into," said Jake. "Good place to raise the kids and it stands to reason you wouldn't have to kill yourself with work. They do farming mostly with machinery and you'd just ride around, steering a tractor or a combine or a baler or something of the sort. Good healthful living, too, out in the sun and open air and you'd get to see some country, more than likely. When the harvest is done the whole kit and caboodle would just pull stakes and go somewhere else. Out to the southwest maybe for the lettuce or the other garden stuff, or out to the coast for fruit or maybe even south. I don't know if there's any winter farming in the south. Maybe you know, Doc."

"No, I don't," said Amby. He sat beside Jake and watched Jake drive; Jake, he admitted to himself, was a fine man at the wheel; a man felt safe and confident with Jake driving. He never went too fast; he took no chances, and he knew how to treat a car.

In the back seat the kids were raising a ruckus, and now Jake turned his attention to them. "If you young'uns don't quiet down, I'm going to stop this here outfit and give you all a hiding. You kids know right well you wouldn't be raising all this rumpus if your Ma was with you instead of back there in the trailer. She'd smack your ears for fair and she'd get you quietened down."

The kids paid no attention, went on with their scuffling.

"I been thinking," Jake said to Amby, his duty as a father now discharged, "that maybe this is the smartest thing you ever done. Maybe you should have done it sooner. Stands to reason an educated man like you won't have no trouble finding a good place in one of these here camps. Ain't likely they got many educated men and there's nothing, I've always said, like an education. Never got one myself and maybe that's why I set such a store by it. One of the things I hated back there in the city was watching them kids run wild without a lick of learning. Myrt and me did the best we could, but neither of us know much more than our ABC's and we weren't proper teachers."

"They probably have schools in all the camps," said Amby. "I've never heard they had, but they have some sort of universities—and before anyone could go to college he'd have to have some sort of elementary education. I rather imagine we'll find the camps equipped with a fair communal program. A camp is a sort of mobile village and more than likely it would be run like one, with schools and hospitals and churches and all the other things you'd expect to find in towns—although all of them, I imagine, will have certain overtones of trade unionism. Culture is a strange thing, Jake, but it usually spells out to pretty much the same in the end result. Differing cultures are no more than different approaches to a common problem."

"I declare," said Jake, "it's a pleasure just to sit here and listen to all that lingo that you throw around. And the beauty of it is you sound just like you know what all them big words mean."

He swung the car off the highway onto the rutted road that ran up to the camp. He slowed to a crawl and they bumped along.

"Look at it," he said. "Ain't it a pretty sight. See all that washing hung out on the lines and those posies growing in the window boxes on the trailers and that little picket fence some of the folks have set up around the trailers, just like the yards back home. I wouldn't be none surprised, Doc, if we find these folks people just like us."

THEY REACHED the camp and swung out of the road, off to one side of the trailers. A crowd of children had gathered and stood watching them. A woman came to the door of one of the trailers and stood, leaning against the doorway, staring at them. Some dogs joined the children and sat down to scratch fleas.

Jake got out of the car. "Hello, kids," he said.

They giggled shyly at him.

Jake's kids piled out of the back seat and stood in a knot beside their father.

Myrt climbed down out of the trailer. She fanned herself with a piece of cardboard. "Well, I never," she declared.

They waited.

Finally an old man came around the end of one of the trailers and walked toward them. The kids parted their ranks to let him through. He walked slowly, with a cane to help him. "Something I can do for you, stranger?"

"We was just looking around," said Jake.

"Look all you want," the oldster told him.

He glanced at Amby, still sitting in the car. "Howdy, old timer."

"Howdy," said Amby.

"Looking for anything special, old timer?"

"I guess you could say we are looking for a job; we hope to find a camp that will take us on."

The old man shook his head.

"We're pretty well full up. But you better talk to the business agent; he's the one to see."

He turned and yelled to the group of staring kids. "You kids go and hunt up Fred."

They scattered like frightened partridges.

"We don't get many folks like you any more," the old man said. "Years ago there were lots of them, just drifting along, looking for whatever they could find. A lot of folks from the smaller towns and a lot of them DF's."

He saw the look of question on Amby's face.

"Displaced farmers," he said. "Ones who couldn't make a go of it and once they took off parity there were a lot of them. Maddest bunch you ever saw. Fighting mad, they were. Had come to count on parity; thought they had it coming to them. Figured the government had done them dirt and I suppose it had. But it did dirt to a lot of the rest of us as well. You couldn't bust things up the way they were busted up without someone getting hurt. And the way things were, you couldn't expect the government to keep on with all their programs. Had to simplify."

Amby nodded in agreement. "You couldn't maintain a top-heavy bureaucracy in a system that had become a technological tribal system."

"I guess you're right," the old man agreed in turn. "So far as the farmers were concerned, it didn't make much difference anyhow. The small land holdings were bound to disappear. The little farmer just couldn't make the grade. Agriculture was on its way toward corporate holdings even before D.C. Machinery was the thing that did it. You couldn't farm without machinery and it didn't pay to buy machinery to handle the few acres on the smaller farms."

HE WALKED closer to the car and stroked one fender with a gnarled hand. "Good car you got here."

"Had it for a long time," Amby told him. "Took good care of it."

The old man brightened. "That's a rule we got around here, too. Everyone has to take good care of everything. Ain't like it was one time when, if you busted something, or it wore out, or you lost it, you could run down to the corner and get another one. Pretty good camp that way. Young fellers spend a whole lot of their spare time dinging up the cars. You should see what they've done to some of them. Yes, sir, there's some of them cars they've made almost human."

He walked up to the open car window and leaned on the door. "Darn good camp," he said. "Anyway you look at it. We got the neatest crops around; and we take good, good care of the soil; and that's worth a lot to the *stuffy* who owns the place. We been coming back to this same place every spring for almost twenty years. If someone beats us here, the *stuffy* won't even talk to them. He always waits for us. There ain't many camps, I can tell you, that can say as much. Of course, in the winter we wander around considerable but that's because we want to. There ain't a winter place we been we couldn't go back to anytime we wanted."

He eyed Amby speculatively. "You wouldn't know nothing about rain-making, now would you?"

"Some years ago I did some reading on what had been done about it," Amby told him. "Cloud seeding, they called it. But I forget what they used. Silver-something. Some kind of chemical."

"I don't know anything about this seeding," the old man said; "and I don't know if they use chemicals or not."

"Of course," he said, anxious not to be misunderstood, "we got a bunch of the finest rain-makers that you ever saw, but in this farming business you can't have too many of them. Better to have one or two too many than one or two too few."

He looked up at the sky. "We don't need no rain right now and it ain't right to use the power, of course, unless you have some need of it. I wish you'd come when we needed rain, for then you could stay over and see the boys in action. They put on quite a show. When they put on a dance everyone turns out to watch."

"I read somewhere once," said Amby, "about the Navahos. Or maybe it was the Hopis…"

But the old man wasn't interested in Navahos or Hopis. "We got a fine crew of green-thumbers, too," he said. "I don't want to sound like bragging, but we got the finest crew…"

The children came charging around the parked trailers, yelling. The old man swung around. "Here comes Fred."

Fred ambled toward them. He was a big man, bareheaded, with an unruly thatch of black hair, bushy eyebrows, a mouthful of white teeth. "Hello, folks," he said. "What can I do for you?"

Jake explained.

FRED SCRATCHED his head, embarrassed and perplexed. "We're full up right now; fact is, we're just on the edge of swarming. I don't see how we can take on another family. Not unless you could offer something special."

"I'm handy at machinery," Jake told him; "I can drive anything."

"We got a lot of drivers. How about repair? Know anything about welding? Can you operate a lathe?"

"Well, no…"

"We have to repair our own machines and keep them in top running shape. Sometimes we have to make parts to replace ones that have been broken. Just can't wait to get replacements from the factory, we're kind of jacks-of-all-trades around here. There's a lot more to it than driving. Anyone can drive. Even the women and the kids."

"Doc here," said Jake, "is an educated man. Was a professor at the university until the university shut down. Maybe you could find some use…"

Fred cheered up. "You don't say. Not agronomy…"

"History," Amby told him, "I don't know anything but history."

"Now that's too bad," said Fred. "We could use an agronomist. We're trying to run some experimental plots, but we don't know too much about it. We don't seem to get nowhere."

The old man looked at Amby and said, "The idea is to develop better strains. It's our stock in trade. One of our better bargaining points. Each camp furnishes its own seed and you can get a better deal out of the *stuffy* if you have top-notch strains. We got a good durham, but we're working on corn now. If we could get some that matured ten days sooner, say…"

"It sounds interesting," said Amby, "but I couldn't help you. I don't know a thing about it."

"I'd sure work hard." said Jake, "if you just gave me a chance. You wouldn't find a more willing worker in your entire camp."

"Sorry," the business agent told him. "We all are willing workers. If you're looking for a place your best bet would be a swarm. They might take you in. An old camp like us don't take newcomers as a rule; not unless they got something special."

"Well," said Jake, "I guess that's it."

He opened the door and got into the car. The kids swarmed into the back seat. Myrt climbed back into the trailer.

"Thanks," Jake said to the business agent. "Sorry we took

up your time."

He swung the car around and bumped back to the road. He was silent for a long time. Finally he spoke up. "What the hell," he asked, "is an agronomist?"

CHAPTER EIGHT

THAT WAS the way it was everywhere they went:

—*Are you one of these cybernetic fellows? No? Too bad. We sure could use one of those cybernetic jerks.*

—*Too bad. We could use a chemist. Messing around with fuels. Don't know a thing except what we dig out. One of these days the boys will blow the whole camp plumb to hell.*

—*Now if you were a lifter. We could use a lifter.*

—*You know electronics, maybe. No? Too bad.*

—*History. Afraid we got no use for history.*

—*You know any medicine? Our Doc is getting old.*

—*Rocket engineer? We got some ideas. We need a guy like that.*

—*History? Nope. What would we do with history?*

But there was a use for history, Amby told himself. "I know there is a use for it," he said. "It has always been a tool before. Now, suddenly, even in a raw, new society such as this, it could not have lost its purpose."

He lay in his sleeping bag and stared up at the sky.

Back home, he thought, it was already autumn; the leaves were turning and the city, in the blaze of autumn, he recalled, was a place of breathless beauty.

But here, deep in the south, it still was summer and there was a queer, lethargic feel to the deep green of the foliage and the flint hard blueness of the sky—as if the green and blue were stamped upon the land and would remain forever, a land where change had been outlawed and the matrix of existence had been hardcast beyond any chance of alteration.

The trailer loomed black against the sky; now that Jake

and Mryt had quit their mumbling talk inside of it, he could hear the purling of the stream that lay just beyond the campsite. The campfire had died down until it was no more than a hint of rose in the whiteness of the ash, and from the edge of the woods a bird struck up a song—a mocking bird, he thought, although not so sweet a song as he had imagined a mocking bird would sing.

That was the way it was with everything, he thought. Nothing was the way you imagined it. Most often a thing would be less glamorous and more prosaic than one had imagined it; and then suddenly, in some unexpected place one would encounter something that would root him in his tracks.

The camps, once he'd seen two or three of them had fallen into pattern—good solid American, sound business-practice patterns; the peculiarities had ceased to be peculiarities once he had come to understand the reason for them.

Like the weekly military drills, for instance, and the regular war games, with every man-Jack of the camp going through maneuvers or working out in all seriousness grimly, without any horseplay, a military problem with the women and the children scattering like coveys of quail to seek out hiding places from imaginary foes.

And that was why, he knew, the federal government could get along on its trifling defense tax. For here, at hand, subject to instantaneous call, was a citizen soldiery that would fight a total, terrible war such as would rip to pieces and hunt down with frontier efficiency and Indian savagery any enemy that might land upon the continent. The federal government maintained the air force, supplied the weapons, conducted the military research and provided the overall command and planning. The people, down to the last and least of them, were the standing army, ready for instant mobilization, trained to hair-trigger readiness, and operative without a dime of federal cost.

It was a setup, he realized now, having seen the war games and the drill that would give pause to any potential enemy. It was something new in the science of warfare. Here stood a nation that presented no target worth the bomb that might be dropped upon it, fostering no cities to be seized and held, no industries that might be ravaged in their entirety, and with every male inhabitant between the ages of 16 and 70 a ready, willing fighter.

He lay there, pondering the many things he'd seen, the strangely familiar and the unfamiliar.

Like the folkways that had grown up within each camp, compounded of legend, superstition, magic, remembered teachings, minor hero-worship and all the other inevitable odds and ends of close communal living. And the folkways, he realized, were a part of the fierce, partisan loyalty of each man and woman for their own home camp. Out of this had arisen the fantastic rivalry, hard at times to understand, which existed among the camps, manifesting itself all the way from the bragging of the small fry to the stiff-necked refusal of camp leaders to share their knowledge or their secrets with any other camp. Hard to understand, all of it, until one saw in it the translation of the old tradition that had been the soul and body of American business practice.

A QUEER layout, thought Dr. Ambrose Wilson, lying in his sleeping bag in the depth of southern night—a queer layout, but a most effective one, and understandable within its terms of reference.

Understandable except for one thing—something on which he could not lay a finger. A feeling, perhaps, rather than a fact—a feeling that somewhere, somehow, underneath this whole new fabric of the neo-gypsy life, lay some new factor, vital and important, that one could sense but could never lay a name to.

He lay there, thinking of that new and vital factor, trying to sift out and winnow the impressions and the clues. But there was nothing tangible; nothing to reach out and grasp; nothing that one could identify. It was like chaff without a single grain, like smoke without a fire—it was something new and, like all the other things, perhaps, entirely understandable within its frame of reference. But where was the reference, he wondered.

They had come down across the land, following the great river, running north to south, and they'd found many camps—crop camps with great acreage's of grain and miles of growing corn; industrial camps with smoking chimneys and the clanking of machines; transportation camps with the pools of trucks and the fantastic operation of a vast freightage web; dairy camps with herds of cattle and the creameries and cheese factories where the milk was processed and the droves of hogs that were a sideline to the dairying; chicken camps; truck farming camps; mining camps; road maintenance camps; lumbering camps and all the others. And now and then the floaters and the swarms, wanderers like themselves, looking for a place.

Everywhere they'd gone it had been the same. A chorus of "too bad" resounding down the land, the swarms of staring children and the scratching dogs and the business agent saying there was nothing.

Some camps had been friendlier than others; in some of these they'd stayed for a day or week to rest up from their travels, to overhaul the motor, to get the kinks out of their legs, to do some visiting.

In those camps he had walked about and talked, sitting in the sun or shade, as the time of day demanded; it had seemed at times he had got to know the people. But always, when it seemed that he had got to know them, he'd sense the subtle strangeness, the nebulous otherness, as if there were someone he could not see sitting in the circle, someone staring at him from some hidden spying spot; and he'd know then that there lay between him and these people a finely-spun fabric of forty years forgotten.

HE LISTENED to their radios, communal versions of the 1960 ham outfits, and heard the ghostly voices come in from other camps, some nearby, some a continent away, a network of weird communication on the village level. Gossip, mostly; but not entirely gossip, for some of it was official messages— the placing of an order for a ton of cheese or a truckload of hay, or the replacement for some broken machine part or possibly the confirmation of a debt that one camp owed another for some merchandise or product, and oftentimes a strange shuffling of those debts from one camp to another, promise paying promise. And what of it was gossip had a special sense, imprinted with the almost unbelievable pattern of this fantastic culture, which overnight had walked out of its suburbia to embrace nomadism.

And always there was magic, a strangely gentle magic used for the good of people rather than their hurt. It was, he thought, as if the brownies and the fairies had come back again after their brief banishment from a materialistic world. There were quaint new ceremonies drawing from the quaintness of the old; there were good-luck charms and certain words to say; there was a resurgence of old and simple faith forgotten in the most recent of our yesterdays, an old and simple faith in certain childish things. *And, perhaps,* he thought, *it is well that it is so.*

But the most puzzling of all was the blending of the ancient magic and the old beliefs with an interest just as vital in modern technology—cybernetics going hand in hand with the good luck charm, the rain dance and agronomy crouching side by side.

All of it bothered him in more ways than one as he sought an understanding of it, tried to break down the pattern and graph it mentally on a historic chart sheet; for as often as the graph seemed to work out to some sensible system it would be knocked out of kilter by the realization he was working with no more than surface evidence.

There was always something missing—that sensed and vital factor.

They had traveled down the continent to a chorus of "too bad." Jake, he knew, was a worried man, as he had every right to be. Lying in his sleeping bag night after night, he'd listened to them talking—Jake and Myrt—when the kids had been asleep and he should have been. And while he'd taken care, out of decency, not to be close enough or listen hard enough to catch their actual words, he had gathered from the tones of their mumbling voices what they had talked about.

It was a shame, he thought; Jake's hopes had been so high and his confidence so great. It was a terrible thing, he told himself, to see a man lose his confidence, a little day by day—to see it drain away from him like blood-drip from a wound.

He stirred, settling his body into the sleeping bag, and shut his eyes against the stars. He felt sleep advance upon him like an ancient comforter; and in that hazy moment he had drifted from the world and yet not entirely lost it, he saw once again, idealized and beautiful, the painting that hung above the fireplace, with the lamplight falling on it.

CHAPTER NINE

THE TRAILER was gone when he awoke. He did not realize it at first, for he lay warm and comfortable, with the fresh wind of morning at his face, listening to the gladness of the birds from each tree and thicket, and the talking of the brook as it flowed among its pebbles.

He lay thinking how fine it was to be alive and vaguely wondering what the day would bring and thankful that he did not fear to meet it.

It was not until then that he saw the trailer was no longer there; he lay quietly for a moment, uncomprehending, before the force of what had happened slapped him in the face.

The first wave of panic washed over him and swiftly ebbed away—the cold fear of aloneness, the panic of desertion—retreating before the dull red glow of anger. He found his clothes inside the sleeping bag and swiftly scrambled out. Sitting on the bag to dress, he took in the scene arid tried to reconstruct how it might have happened.

The camp lay just beyond a long dip in the road and he remembered how they had blocked the trailer's wheels against the slope of ground. More than likely Jake had simply taken away the blocks, released the brakes, and rolled down the hill, not starting the motor until well out of hearing.

He got up from the sleeping bag and walked numbly forward. Here were the stones they'd used to block the trailer and there the tracks of the tires straight across the dew.

And something else: Leaning against a tree was the .22 rifle that had been Jake's most prized possession and beside it an old and bulging haversack.

He knelt beside the tree and unstrapped the haversack. There were two cartons of matches, ten boxes of ammunition, his extra clothing, food, cooking and eating utensils, and an old raincoat.

He knelt there, looking at it all spread upon the ground and he felt the burning of the tears just behind his eyelids. Treachery, sure—but not entirely treacherous, for they'd not forgotten him. Thievery and desertion and the worst of bad intentions, yet Jake had left him the rifle that had been his good right arm.

Those mumbled conversations that he had listened to— could they have been plotting rather than just worried talk? And what if he had listened to the words rather than the mumble, what if he had crept and listened and learned what they were planning—what could he have done about it?

He repacked the haversack and carried it and the rifle to his sleeping bag. It would be a lot to carry, but he would take it slow and easy and he would get along. As a matter of fact, he consoled himself, he was not too badly off; he still had his billfold and the money that remained. He wondered, without caring much, how Jake, without a cent, would get gasoline and food when he needed it.

And he could hear Jake saying, in those mumbled nightly talks: *"It's Doc. That's why they won't take us in. They take one look at him and know the day is not far off when he'll be a welfare charge. They aren't taking on someone who'll be a burden to them in a year or two."*

Or: *"It's Doc, I tell you. Myrt. He flings them big words around and they are scared of him. Figure he won't fit. Figure he is snooty. Now take us. We're common, ordinary folks. They'd take us like a shot if we weren't packing Doc."*

Or: *"Now us, we can do any kind of work, but Doc is specialized. We won't get nothing unless we cut loose from Doc."*

Amby shook his head. It was funny, he thought, to what lengths a man would go once he got desperate enough. Gratitude and honor, even friendship, were frail barriers to the actions of despair.

And I, he asked himself.

What do I do now?

Certainly not the first thing that had popped into his head—turning around and heading back for home. That would be impossible; in another month or so, snow would have fallen in the north and he would be unable to get through. If he decided to go home, he'd have to wait till spring.

There was one thing to do—continue southward, traveling as he had been traveling, but at a slower pace. There might even be some merit in it. He would be by himself and would have more time to think. And here was a situation that called for a lot of thinking, a lot of puzzling out. Somewhere, he knew, there had to be an answer and a key to that factor he had sensed within the camps. Once he had that factor, the history graph could be worked out, and he would have done the task he had set out to do.

He left the haversack and rifle on the sleeping bag and walked out to the road. He stood in the middle of it, looking first one way and then the other. It was a long and lonely road and he must travel it as lonely as the road. He'd never had a child, and of recent years he'd scarcely had a friend. Jake, he admitted now, had been his closest friend; but Jake was gone, cut off from him not only by the distance and the winding road, but by this act which now lay between them.

He squared his shoulders, with an outward show of competence and bravery which he did not feel, and walked back to pick up the sleeping bag, the haversack and rifle.

CHAPTER TEN

IT WAS A month later that he stumbled on the truckers' camp, quite by accident.

It was coming on toward evening; he was on the lookout for a place to spend the night when he approached the intersection and saw the semi-trailer parked there.

A man was squatted beside a newly lighted campfire, carefully feeding small sticks to the flame. A second man was unpacking what appeared to be a grub-box. A third was coming out of the woods with a bucket, probably carrying water from a nearby stream.

The man tending the fire saw Amby, and stood up. "Howdy, stranger," he called. "Looking for a place to camp?"

Amby nodded and approached the campfire. He took the haversack and sleeping bag off his shoulder and dropped them to the ground. "I'd be much obliged."

"Glad to have you," said the man. He hunkered down beside the fire again and went on nursing it. "Ordinarily we don't camp out for the night. We just stop long enough to cook a bite to eat, then hit the road again. We got a bunk in the job so one of us can sleep while another drives. Even Tom has got so he's pretty good at driving."

He nodded at the man who had brought in the water.

"Tom ain't a trucker. He's a perfesser at a university, on a leave of absence."

Tom grinned across the fire at Amby. "Sabbatical."

"So am I," said Amby. "Mine is permanent."

"But tonight we'll make a night of it," went on the trucker. "I don't like the sound of the motor. She's heating up some, too. We'll have to tear it down."

"Tear it down right here?"

"Why not? Good a place as any."

"But…"

The trucker chuckled. "We'll get along all right. Jim, my helper over there—he's a lifter. He'll just h'ist her out and bring her over to the fire and we'll tear her down."

Amby sat down by the fire. "I'm Amby Wilson," he said. "Just wandering around."

"Rambling far?"

"From up in Minnesota."

"Far piece of walking for a man your age."

"I came part of the way by car."

"Car break down on you?"

"My partner ran off with it."

"Now," the trucker said, judiciously, "that's what I'd call a lousy, lowdown trick."

"Jake didn't mean any harm; he just got panicky."

"You try to track him down?"

"What's the use of trying? There's no way that I can."

"You could get a tracer."

"What's a tracer?"

"Pop," the trucker asked, "where the hell you been?"

And it was a fair question, Amby admitted to himself.

"A tracer," said Tom, "is a telepath. A special kind of telepath. He can track down a mind and find it almost every time. A kind of human bloodhound. It's hard work and there aren't many of them; but as the years go by we hope there will be more and better."

A tracer is a telepath!

Just like that, without any warning.

A special kind of telepath—as if there might be many

other kinds of them.

AMBY SAT hunched before the fire and looked cautiously around to catch the sheltered grin. But they were not grinning; they acted, he thought, as if this matter of a telepath was very commonplace.

Could it be that here, he wondered, within minutes after meeting them, these people had been the first to say the word that made some sense out of the welter of folklore and magic he'd encountered in the camps?

A tracer was a telepath; and a lifter might be a teleporter; and a green-thumber very well might be someone who had an inherent, exaggerated sympathy and understanding for the world of living things.

Was this, then, the missing factor he had sought; the differentness sensed in the camps; the logic behind the rainmakers and all the other mumbo-jumbo that he had thought of as merely incidental to an enclosed social group?

He brought his hands together between his knees, locking his fingers together tightly, to keep from trembling. *Good Lord, he thought, if this is it, so many things explained! If this is the answer that I sought, then here is a culture that is unbeatable!*

Tom broke in upon his thinking. "You said you were on a sabbatical as well as I. A permanent one, you said. Are you a school man, too?"

"I was," said Amby, "but the university closed down. It was one of the old universities, and there was no money and not many students."

"You're looking for another school post?"

"I'd take anything; it seems that no one wants me."

"The schools are short on men. They would snap you up."

"You mean these trailer universities."

Tom nodded. "That is what I mean."

"You don't think much of them?" the trucker asked, his hackles rising.

"I don't know anything about them."

"They're good as any schools there ever were," the trucker said. "Don't let no one tell you different."

Amby hunched forward toward the fire, the many questions, the hope and fear bubbling in his mind. "This tracer business," he said. "You said a tracer was a special kind of telepath. Are there others—I mean, are there other possibilities?"

"Some," said Tom. "There seems to be a lot of special talent showing up these days. We catch a lot of them in the universities and we try to train them, but there isn't much that we can do. After all, how could you or I train a telepath? How would you go about it? About the best that we can do is to encourage each one of them to use such talent as he has to the best advantage."

Amby shook his head, confused. "But I don't understand. Why do you have them now when we never used to have them?"

"Perhaps there may have been some of them before D. C. There must have been, for the abilities must have been there, latent, waiting for their chance. But maybe, before this, they never had a chance. Maybe they were—well, killed in the rush. Or the abilities that there were may have been smothered under the leveling influence of the educational system. There may have been some who had the talents, and were afraid to use them for fear of being different in a culture where differentness was something to point a finger at. And being afraid, they suppressed them, until they weren't bothered by them. And there may have been others who used their talents secretly to their own advantage. Can you imagine what a lawyer or a politician or a salesman could have done with telepathy?"

"You believe this?"

"Well, not all of it. But the possibilities exist."

"What do you believe then?"

"Folks are smarter now," the trucker said.

"No, Ray, that isn't it at all. The people are the same. Perhaps there were special talents back before D. C., but I don't think they showed up as often as they show up now. We got rid of a whole lot of the older restrictions and conventionalities. We threw away a lot of the competition and the pressure when we left the houses, and all the other things we had thought we couldn't get along without. We cut out the complexities. Now no one is breathing down our necks. We don't have to worry so much about keeping up with the man next door—because the man next door has become a friend and is no longer a yardstick of our social and economic station. We aren't trying to pack forty-eight hours of living into every twenty-four. Maybe we're giving ourselves the chance to develop what we missed before."

JIM, THE helper, had hung a pot of coffee on a forged stick over the fire and now was cutting meat.

"Pork chops tonight," said Ray, the trucker. "We were passing by a farm camp this morning and there was this pig out in the road and there wasn't nothing I could do…"

"You almost wrecked the truck to get him."

"Now, that's a downright libel," Ray protested. "I did my level best to miss him."

Jim went on cutting chops, throwing them into a big frying pan as he sliced them off.

"If you're looking for a teaching job," said Tom, "all you got to do is go to one of the universities. There are a lot of them. Most of them not large."

"But where do I find them?"

"You'd have to ask around. They moved around a lot.

Get tired of one place and go off to another. But you're lucky now. The south is full of them. Go north in the spring, come south in the fall."

The trucker had settled back on his haunches and was building himself a cigarette. He lifted the paper to his mouth and licked it, twirling it in shape. He stuck it in his mouth and it drooped there limply while he hunted for a small twig from the fire to give himself a light.

"Tell you what," he said, "why don't you just come along with us? There's room for everyone. Bound to find a bunch of universities along the way. You can have your pick of them. Or you might take it in your mind to stick with us right out to the coast. Tom is going out there to see some shirt-tail relatives of his."

Tom nodded. "Sure. Why don't you come along."

"Ain't like it was in the old days," said the trucker. "My old man was a trucker then. You went hell-for-leather. You didn't stop for nothing—not even to be human. You just kept rolling."

"That was the way with all of us," said Amby.

"Now we take it easy," said the trucker. "We don't get there as fast, but we have a lot more fun and there ain't no one suffering if we're late a day or two."

Jim put the pan of chops on the bed of coals.

"It's a lot easier trucking, too," said Ray, "if you can get a lifter for a helper. Nothing to loading or unloading if you have a lifter. And if you get stuck in the mud, he can push you out. Jim here is the best lifter that I ever saw. He can lift that big job if he has to without any trouble. But you got to keep after him; he's the laziest mortal I ever saw."

Jim went on frying chops.

The trucker flipped the cigarette toward the fire and it landed in the pan of chops. Almost immediately it rose out of them; described a tiny arc and fell into the coals.

Jim said: "Ray, you got to cut out things like that. Watch what you are doing. You wear me out just picking up behind you."

The trucker said to Amby, "How about joining up with us? You'd see a lot of country."

Amby shook his head. "I'll have to think about it."

But he was dissembling. He didn't have to think about it.

He knew he wasn't going.

CHAPTER ELEVEN

HE STOOD by the dead campfire at the intersection and waved goodbye to them, watching the semi-trailer disappear down the road in the early morning mist.

Then he bent down and picked up the haversack and the sleeping bag and slung them on his shoulder.

He felt within himself a strange urgency—a happy urgency. And it was fine to feel it once again after all these months. Fine again to know he had a job to do.

He stood for a moment, staring around at the camping grounds—the dead ash of the fire, the pile of unused wood, and the great spot on the ground where the grease from the motor of the truck soaked slowly in the soil.

He would not have believed it, he knew, if he had not seen it done—seen Jim lift the motor from the truck once the bed bolts had been loosened, lift it and guide it to rest beside the fire without once laying hands upon it. Again he had watched the stubborn nuts that defied the wrench turn slowly and reluctantly without a tool upon them, then spin freely to rise free of the thread and deposit themselves neatly in a row.

Once, long ago it seemed, he'd talked with a *stuffy* who had told him how efficiently a camp had run his plant, complaining all the while of how they'd rejiggered it until it would take any other camp a month at least to figure out the sheer mechanics of it.

Efficient! Good Lord, of course they were efficient! What new methods, what half-guessed new principles, he wondered, may have gone into that rejiggered plant?

All over the country, he wondered, how many new principles and methods might there be at work? But not regarded as new principles by the camps that had worked them out; regarded rather as trade secrets, as powerful points in bargaining, as tribal stock-in-trade. And in the whole country, he wondered, how many new talents might there be, how many applicable variations of those specific talents.

A new culture, he thought—an unbeatable culture if it only knew its strength, if it could be jarred out of its provincialism, if it could strip from its new abilities the veil of superstition. And that last, he knew, might be the toughest job off all; the magic had been used to cloak annoying ignorance and as an explanation for misunderstanding. It offered a simple and an easy explanation, and it might be hard to substitute in its stead the realization that at the moment there could be little actual knowledge and no complete understanding only an acceptance and a patience against the day when it might be understood.

He walked over to the tree where he had leaned his rifle and picked it up. He swung it almost gaily in his hand and was astonished at the familiarity of it, almost as if it were a part of him, an extension of his hand.

And that was the way it was with these people and the possibilities. They'd gotten so accustomed to the magic, that it had become a part of everyday; they did not see the greatness if it.

THE POSSIBILITIES, once one thought of them, were fantastic. Develop the abilities and within another hundred years the sputtering radios would be gone, replaced by telepaths who would blanket the nation with a flexible network of communications that never would break down, that would be immune to atmospheric conditions—an intelligent, human system of communication without the inherent limitations of an electronic setup.

The trucks would be gone, too, with relays of teleporters whisking shipments from coast to coast (and all points in between), fast and smooth and without a hitch and, once again, without regard to weather or to road conditions.

And that was only two facets of the picture. What of all the others—the known, the suspected, the now-impossible?

He walked from the campsite out to the road and stood for a moment, wondering. Where was that camp where they had asked if he was a rocket engineer? And where had been the camp that had been in the market for a chemist because the boys were fooling around with fuels? And where, he wondered, would he be able to pick up a lifter? And perhaps a good, all-purpose telepath.

It wasn't much, this thing he had in mind, he admitted to himself. But it was a start. "Give me ten years," he said. "Just ten years is all I ask."

But even if he had no more than two, he had to make a start. For if he made the start, then perhaps there'd be someone who would carry on. Someone had to make a start. Someone like himself, perhaps, who could look upon this neo-tribal world objectively and in the light of the historic past. *And there may not he many of us left,* he thought.

He might have a hard job selling them, he knew, but he thought he knew the pitch.

He set off up the road and he whistled as he went.

It wasn't much, but it would be spectacular if he could accomplish it. Once it had been done, it would be a thing that every camp would spy and scheme and cheat and steal to do.

And it would take something such as that, he knew, to knock some sense into their heads; to make them see the possibilities; to set them to wondering how they might turn to use the other strange abilities, which had blossomed here in the soil of a new society.

Now where was that camp where they'd been in need of a rocket engineer?

Up the road somewhere. Up the winding, lonely road that was no longer lonely.

Just up the road apiece. A hundred miles or two. Or was it more than that?

He jogged along, trying to remember. But it was hard to remember. There had been so many days and so many camps. A landmark, he thought—I was always good at landmarks.

But there had been too many landmarks, too.

CHAPTER TWELVE

HE WANDERED up the road, stopping at the camps and the answer that he got became monotonous.

"Rockets? Hell, no! Who'd fool around with rockets?"

And he wondered: Had there ever been a camp where they'd said they could use a rocket engineer? Who would fool around with rockets? What would be the use of it?

The word went ahead of him, by telepathy perhaps, by radio, by fast-running word of mouth, and he found himself a legend. He found them waiting for him, as if they had been expecting him, and they had a standard greeting that soon became a joke.

"You the gent who's looking for the rockets?"

But with their joking and the legend of him, he became one of them; and yet, even in becoming one of them, he still stood apart from them and saw the greatness that they missed, a greatness that they had to—*had to*—be awakened to. And a greatness that mere words and preaching would never make come alive for them.

He sat at the nightly communal gabfests, slept in those trailers that had room for an extra person, and helped at little tasks and listened to the yarning. And in turn did some yarning of his own. Time after time he felt again the strangeness and the otherness; but now that he recognized it, it did not disturb him—and sometimes, looking around the circle, he could spot the one who had it.

Lying in a bunk at night, before he went to sleep, he thought a lot about it and finally it all made sense to him.

These abilities had been with Man always, perhaps even from the caves, but then, as now, Man had not understood the power and so had not followed it. Rather he had followed along another path—ignoring mind for hand—and had built himself a wonderful and impressive and complex culture of machines. He'd built with his hands and with mighty labor the vast, complex machines, which did what he might have done with the power of mind alone had he but chosen to do so. Rather he had hidden the mental power behind semantics of his own devising, and in seeking after intellectual status had laughed into disrepute the very thing he sought.

This thing which had happened, Amby told himself, was no quirk in the development of the race, but as sure and certain as the sun. It was no more than a returning to the path it had been intended all along that Man should follow. After centuries of stumbling, the human race once more was headed right again. And even if there had been no decentralization, no breakup of the culture, it would eventually have happened, for somewhere along the line of technology there must be a breakdown point. Machines could only get so big. There had to be an end somewhere to complexity, be it in machines or living.

Decentralization may have helped a little, might have hurried the process along by a thousand years or so, but that was all it amounted to.

And here once again Man had devised clever words—commonplace words—to dim the brightness of this frightening thing he could not understand. A teleporter was called a lifter; a telepath a tracer or a talker, the ability to follow worldliness a bit into the future was called second sight, while one who practiced it was usually called a peeker. And there were many other abilities, too—unrecognized or little better than half-guessed—all lumped under the general term of magic. But this did not matter greatly. A common and a homey word served just as well as correct terminology, and might even in the end lead to a readier acceptance. The thing that did matter greatly was that this time the abilities not be lost and not be pushed aside. Something would happen, something had to happen, to shock these people into a realization of what they really had.

So he went from camp to camp and now there was no need to ask the question, for the question went before him.

He went along the roads, a legend, and now he heard of another legend, a man who went from camp to camp dispensing medicines and cures.

IT WAS ONLY a rumor at first, heard oftener and oftener; finally he found a camp where the healer had stopped no more than a week before. Sitting around a campfire that evening, he listened to the wonder of the healer.

"Mrs. Cooper complained for years," an old crone told him. "Was sickly all the time. Kept to her bed for days. Couldn't keep nothing on her stomach. Then she took one bottle of this stuff and you should see her now. Sprightly as a jay."

Across the fire an old man nodded gravely. "I had rheumatiz," he said. "Just couldn't seem to shake it. Misery in my bones all the blessed time. The camp doc, he couldn't do a thing. Got a bottle of this stuff..."

He got up and danced a limber jig to put across his point.

In not one camp, but twenty, the story was the same—of those who left their beds and walked; of miseries disappeared; of complaints gone overnight.

Another one of them, Amby told himself. Another piece of magic. A man with the art of healing at his fingertips. Where would it end, he wondered.

Then he met the healer.

He came on the deserted camp after dusk had fallen. It was just at the hour when the suppers should be over, and the dishes done, and people would be gathering to sit around and talk. But there was not a soul around the trailers—except a dog or two at the garbage cans—and the streets that ran between the trailers echoed in their emptiness.

He stood in the center of the camp, wondering if he should shout to attract attention, but he was afraid to shout. Slowly he wheeled about, watching narrowly for the slightest motion, for the first pinprick of wrongness. It was then he saw the flare of light at the south edge of the camp.

Advancing cautiously toward it, he caught the murmur of the crowd when he was still a good ways off. He hesitated for a moment, doubtful if he should intrude, then went slowly forward.

The crowd, he saw, was gathered at the edge of a grove just beyond the camp. They were squeezed into a close-packed knot before a solitary trailer. The scene was lighted by a half dozen flares thrust into the ground.

A man stood on the steps that led up to the trailer's door, and his, voice floated faintly to where Amby stood; but faint as the words might be, there was a familiar pattern to them. Amby stood there, thinking back to boyhood, and a small town he had not thought of for years, and the sound of banjo music and the running in the streets. It had been exciting, he remembered, and they'd talked of it for days. Old Lady Adams, he remembered, had sworn by the medicine she'd bought, and waited patiently for years for the medicine show to come back to town again so she could get some more. But it never came again.

He walked forward to the edge of the crowd and a woman turned her head to tell him, whispering fiercely, "It's him!" as if it might be the Lord Almighty. Then she went back to listening.

The man on the steps was in full spiel by this time. He didn't talk so loud, but his voice carried and it had a quietness and a pompous, yet human, authority.

"My friends," he was saying, "I'm just an ordinary man. I wouldn't have you think different. I wouldn't want to fool you by saying I was somebody, because in fact I ain't. I don't even talk so good. I ain't much good at grammar. But maybe there are a lot of the rest of you who don't know much grammar, either, and I guess the most of you can understand me; so it'll be all right. I'd like to come right down there in the crowd and talk to each one of you, face to face, but you can hear me better if I stand up here. I'm not trying to put on any airs by standing up here on these steps. I ain't trying to put myself above you.

"Now I've told you that I wouldn't fool you, not even for a minute. I'd rather cut my tongue out and throw it to the hogs than tell you a thing that wasn't true. So I ain't going to make no high-flown claims for this medicine of mine. I'm going to start right out by being honest with you. I'm going to tell you that I ain't even a doctor. I never studied medicine. I don't know a thing about it. I just like to think of myself as a messenger—someone who is carrying good news.

"There's quite a story connected with this medicine and if you'll just hold still for a while I'd like to tell it to you. It goes a long ways back and some of it sounds almost unbelievable, but I wish you would believe me, for every word is true. First, I'll have to tell you about my old grandma. She's been dead these many years, God rest her. There never was a finer or a kinder woman and I remember when I was just a lad…"

Amby walked back from the crowd a ways and sat down limply on the ground.

The gall of the guy, he thought, the sheer impertinence!

When it was all over, when the last bottle had been sold, when the people had gone back to the camp and the medicine man was gathering up the flares, Amby rose and walked forward.

"Hello, Jake," he said.

CHAPTER THIRTEEN

JAKE SAID, "Well, I tell you, Doc, I was kind of backed against the wall. We was down to nothing. No money for gasoline or grub and begging hadn't been so good. So I got to thinking, sort of desperate like. And I thought that just because a man's been honest all his life doesn't mean he has to keep on being honest. But for the life of me, I couldn't see how I could profit much even from dishonesty, except maybe stealing and that's too dangerous. Although I was ready to do most anything."

"I can believe that," Amby said.

"Aw, Doc," pleaded Jake, "What you keep pouring it on for? There ain't no sense of you staying sore. We was sorry right away we left you; we would have turned around right away and come back again, except that I was scared to. And anyhow, it worked out all right."

He flipped the wheel a little to miss a rock lying in the road.

"Well, sir," he said, continuing with his story, "it does beat all how things will happen. Just when you figure you are sunk, something will turn up. We stopped along this river, you see, to try to catch some fish and the kids found an old dump there and got rooting around in it, the way kids will, you know. And they found a lot of bottles—four or five dozen of them—all of them alike. I imagine someone had hauled them out long ago and dumped them. I sat looking at those bottles, not having much of anything else to do, and I got to wondering if I had any use for them or if it would be just a waste of space hauling them along. Then all of a sudden it hit me just like that. They were all full of dirt and some of them were chipped, but we got them washed and polished up and..."

"Tell me, what did you put in the bottles?"

"Well, Doc, I tell you honest, I just don't remember what I used for that first batch."

"Nothing medicinal, I take it."

"Doc, I wouldn't have the slightest notion of what goes into medicine. The only thing to be careful of is not to put in anything that will kill them or make them very sick. But you got to make it unpleasant or they won't think it's any good. Myrt, she fussed some about it to start with, but she's all right now. Especially since people claim the stuff is doing them some good, although how in the world it could I can't rightly figure out. Doc, how in the world could stuff like that be any good at all?"

"It isn't."

"But folks claim it helps. There was this one old geezer..."

"It's conditioned faith," said Amby. "They're living in a world of magic and they're ready to accept almost anything. They practically beg for miracles."

"You mean it's all in their heads?"

"Every bit of it. These people have all lost their sophistication, or you'd never got away with it; they'll accept a thing like that on faith. They drink the stuff and expect so confidently it will help them that it really does. They haven't been battered since they were old enough to notice with high-power advertising claims. They haven't been fooled time after time by product claims. They haven't been gypped and lied to and cajoled and threatened. So they're ready to believe."

"So that's the way it is," said Jake. "I'm glad to know; I

worried some about it."

THE KIDS were scuffling in the back seat and Jake chewed them out, but the kids went on scuffling. It was like old times again.

Amby settled back comfortably in the seat, watching the scenery go by. "You're sure you know where this camp is?"

"I can see it, Doc, just like it was yesterday. I remember thinking it was funny those guys would need a rocket engineer."

He looked slantwise at Amby. "How come you're in such a lather to find this camp of theirs?"

"I got an idea," Amby told him.

"You know, Doc, I was thinking now that you're back we might team up together. You with your white hair and that big lingo that you use..."

"Forget it," Amby said.

"There ain't no harm in it," protested Jake. "We'd give them a show. That's what brought them out at first. It ain't like it used to be back before D.C. when there was television and the movies and baseball games and such. There ain't much entertainment now and they'd come out just to hear us talk."

Amby didn't answer.

It was good to be back again, he thought. He should be sore at Jake, but somehow he couldn't be. They'd all been so glad to see him—even the kids and Myrt—and they were trying so hard to make up for their deserting him.

And they'd do it all over again if the occasion ever arose where they thought it would be to their advantage; but in the meantime they were good people to be with, and they were heading where he'd wanted to go. He was satisfied. He wondered how long he would have had to hunt before he found the rocket camp if Jake had not turned up again. He wondered, vaguely, if he'd ever found it.

"You know," Jake said, "I been thinking it over and I might just run for congress. This medicine business has given me a lot of practice at public speaking and I know just the plank to run on—abolish this here road tax. I never heard anyone in all my life as burned up at anything as these folks are at the road tax."

"You couldn't run for congress," Amby told him. "You aren't a resident of any place. You don't belong to any camp."

"I never thought of that. Maybe I could join up with some camp long enough to…"

"And you can't abolish the road tax if you want to keep the roads."

"Maybe you're right at that, Doc. But it does seem a shame these folks are pestered by the road tax. It sure has them upset."

He squinted at the dials on the instrument panel. "If we don't have any trouble," he said, "We'll be at that camp of yours by tomorrow evening."

CHAPTER FOURTEEN

THEY SAID, "It won't work." But that was one of the things he had known they'd say.

"It won't work if you don't co-operate," said Amby. "To do it you need fuel."

"We got fuel."

"Not good enough," said Amby; "not nearly good enough. This camp just down the road is working on some fuels."

"You want us to go down there with our hats in hand and..."

"Not with your hats in hand. You have something; they have something. Why don't you make a trade?"

They digested that, sitting in a circle under the big oak tree that grew in the center of the camp. He watched them digesting it—the hard and puzzled faces, the shrewd, nineteenth-century Yankee faces, the grease-grimed hands folded in their laps.

All around were the trailers with their window boxes and their lines of washing, with the women-faces and the children-faces peering out of doors and windows, all being very silent; this was an important council, and they knew their place.

And beyond the trailers the great stacks of the farm machinery plant.

"I tell you, mister," said the business agent. "This rocket business is just a hobby with us. Some of the boys found some books about it and read up a little and got interested. And in a little while the whole camp got interested. We do it like some other camps play baseball or hold shooting matches. We aren't hell-for-leather set on doing something with it. We're just having fun."

"But if you could use the rockets?"

"We ain't prejudiced against using them, but we got to think it through."

"You would need some lifters."

"We've got lifters, mister; we got a lot of them. We pick up all we can. They cut down the operation costs, so we can afford to pay them what they ask. We use a lot of them in the assembly plant."

One of the younger men spoke up. "There's just one thing about it. Can a lifter lift himself?"

"Why couldn't he?"

"Well, you take a piece of pipe. You can pick it up without any trouble, say. But if you stand on it, you can tug your muscles out and you can't even budge it."

"A lifter can lift himself, all right," said the business agent. "We got one fellow in assembly who rides around at work— on the pieces he is lifting. Claims it's faster that way."

"Well, all right, then," said Amby. "Put your lifter in a trailer; he could lift it, couldn't he?"

The business agent nodded. "Easily."

"And handle it? Bring it down again without busting it all up?"

"Sure he could."

"But he couldn't move it far. How far would you say?"

"Five miles, maybe. Maybe even ten. It looks easy, sure, but there's a lot of work to it."

"But if you put rockets on the trailer, then all the lifter would have to do would be to keep it headed right. How hard would that be?"

"Well, I don't rightly know," the business agent said. "But I think it would be easy. He could keep it up all day."

66

"And if something happened? If a rocket burned out, say. He could bring it down to earth without smashing anything."

"I would say he could."

"What are we sitting here for, then?"

"Mister," asked the business agent, "what are you getting at?"

"Flying camps," said Amby. "Can't you see it, man! Want to move somewhere else, or just go on vacation—why, the whole camp would take to the air and be there in no time."

The business agent rubbed his chin. "I don't say it wouldn't work," he admitted. "My guess is that it would. But why should we bother? If we want to go somewhere else we got all the time there is. We ain't in any hurry."

"Yes," said another man, "just tell us one good reason."

"Why, the road tax," Amby said. "If you didn't use the roads, you wouldn't have to pay the tax."

In the utter silence he looked around the circle, and he knew he had them hooked.

THE END

If you've enjoyed this book, you will not want to miss these terrific titles…

ARMCHAIR SCI-FI, FANTASY, & HORROR DOUBLE NOVELS, $12.95 each

If you've enjoyed this book, you will not want to miss these terrific titles…

ARMCHAIR SCI-FI, FANTASY, & HORROR DOUBLE NOVELS, $12.95 each

D-21   **EMPIRE OF EVIL** by Robert Arnette
             THE SIGN OF THE TIGER by Alan E. Nourse & J. A. Meyer

D-22   **OPERATION SQUARE PEG** by Frank Belknap Long
             ENCHANTRESS OF VENUS by Leigh Brackett

D-23   **THE LIFE WATCH** by Lester Del Rey
             CREATURES OF THE ABYSS by Murray Leinster

D-24   **LEGION OF LAZARUS** by Edmond Hamilton
             STAR HUNTER by Andre Norton

D-25   **EMPIRE OF WOMEN** by John Fletcher
             ONE OF OUR CITIES IS MISSING by Irving Cox

D-26   **THE WRONG SIDE OF PARADISE** by Raymond F. Jones
             THE INVOLUNTARY IMMORTALS by Rog Phillips

D-27   **EARTH QUARTER** by Damon Knight
             ENVOY TO NEW WORLDS by Keith Laumer

D-28   **SLAVES TO THE METAL HORDE** by Milton Lesser
             HUNTERS OUT OF TIME by Joseph E. Kelleam

D-29   **RX JUPITER SAVE US** by Ward Moore
             BEWARE THE USURPERS by Geoff St. Reynard

D-30   **SECRET OF THE SERPENT** by Don Wilcox
             CRUSADE ACROSS THE VOID by Dwight V. Swain

ARMCHAIR SCIENCE FICTION CLASSICS, $12.95 each

C-7   **THE SHAVER MYSTERY, pt. 1**
             by Richard S. Shaver

C-8   **THE SHAVER MYSTERY, pt. 2**
             by Richard S. Shaver

C-9   **MURDER IN SPACE** by David V. Reed
             by David V. Reed

ARMCHAIR MASTERS OF SCIENCE FICTION SERIES, $16.95 each

M-3   **MASTERS OF SCIENCE FICTION, Vol. Three**
             Robert Sheckley, "The Perfect Woman" and other tales

M-4   **MASTERS OF SCIENCE FICTION, Vol. Four**
             Mack Reynolds, "Stowaway" and other tales

If you've enjoyed this book, you will not want to miss these terrific titles…

ARMCHAIR SCI-FI & HORROR DOUBLE NOVELS, $12.95 each

D-31   **A HOAX IN TIME** by Keith Laumer
          INSIDE EARTH by Poul Anderson

D-32   **TERROR STATION** by Dwight V. Swain
          THE WEAPON FROM ETERNITY by Dwight V. Swain

D-33   **THE SHIP FROM INFINITY** by Edmond Hamilton
          TAKEOFF by C. M. Kornbluth

D-34   **THE METAL DOOM** by David H. Keller
          TWELVE TIMES ZERO by Howard Browne

D-35   **HUNTERS OUT OF SPACE** by Joseph Kelleam
          INVASION FROM THE DEEP by Paul W. Fairman,

D-36   **THE BEES OF DEATH** by Robert Moore Williams
          A PLAGUE OF PYTHONS by Frederick Pohl

D-37   **THE LORDS OF QUARMALL** by Fritz Leiber and Harry Fischer
          BEACON TO ELSEWHERE by James H. Schmitz

D-38   **BEYOND PLUTO** by John S. Campbell
          ARTERY OF FIRE by Thomas N. Scortia

D-39   **SPECIAL DELIVERY** by Kris Neville
          NO TIME FOR TOFFEE by Charles F. Meyers

D-40   **RECALLED TO LIFE** by Robert Silverberg
          JUNGLE IN THE SKY by Milton Lesser

ARMCHAIR SCIENCE FICTION CLASSICS, $12.95 each

C-10   **MARS IS MY DESTINATION**
          by Frank Belknap Long

C-11   **SPACE PLAGUE**
          by George O. Smith

C-12   **SO SHALL YE REAP**
          by Rog Phillips

ARMCHAIR SCIENCE FICTION & HORROR GEMS SERIES, $12.95 each

G-3   **SCIENCE FICTION GEMS, Vol. Two**
         James Blish and others

G-4   **HORROR GEMS, Vol. Two**
         Joseph Payne Brennan and others

WHEN THE MACHINES TOOK OVER...

Biogenetic advances had made such progress that it was now possible to determine the exact genes and precise nature desirable in the human adult. For the first time in history an individual's instincts could be successfully controlled.

Experience had shown that it was in Society's best interests to maintain, at all times, a perfect balance of the more desirable genetic types... But who got to make these determinations?

John Tabor... marriage privilege denied...

This is a science-fiction thriller about a machine that computed men's futures... and one man who dared to tamper with the unacceptable results...

CAST OF CHARACTERS

JOHN TABOR
He'd spent two years alone on Venus Base, and now, after being rejected for marriage (again!) he was ready to risk anything.

CLAIRE
Although she was John's specifically designed "Biogenetic Norm Woman," she wasn't just your average Stepford wife.

AGNES
Passionate, seductive and ready to fight for exemption, was she really everything she promised?

GIANT SIZE
In a world where good-looking women were scarce he was a big man willing to make big moves…

TOTAL STRANGERS
Who the hell were these people anyway? And how could you trust any promise they might make?

WINNER-TAKE-ALL
In a bicycle race to the death only one man would take the prize, and this cyclist was going for the gold!

THE BIG BRAIN
A computer of unfathomable magnitude. Its job was to decide the fate of humanity—who would procreate, and who would not.

IT WAS THE DAY OF THE DAY OF THE ROBOT

By
FRANK BELKNAP LONG

ARMCHAIR FICTION
PO Box 4369, Medford, Oregon 97504

CHAPTER ONE

YOU STAND before the humming computers and you fight off terror. You feel a more-than-human wisdom crushing you to the earth, denying you the right to think for yourself. You know that the future should be in your own hands, but you can't wring that much independence of thought and action from the master controls.

The Big Brain can't know what a man is thinking, but the feeling is there—the guilt feeling. You want to escape but can't. You look around you and see your own face mirrored back. You see on gleaming metal the haggard eyes and tight, despairing lips of a total stranger.

The girl at my side was trembling violently. She'd punched her identity number, and the Big Brain's answer had struck her like a hard-knuckled hand in the dark.

I could see the punched metaltape gleaming on her palm—four inches of tape. I could see the torment in her eyes, the film of moisture she was furiously trying to blink away. She was staring straight at me, but I knew my face meant nothing to her. It could only have seemed the cold face of a stranger, trapped like herself.

The realization of her torment gave a sharp, heady quality to my anger. The guilt feeling dissolved and I felt only anger. She was so very beautiful that I succumbed to the universal human fantasy, I saw her as an outcast girl in a freedom ruin and there was the tang of death in the air and the rich, heavy perfume which outcast women wore.

She was standing against a crumbling stone wall, her large, dark eyes wide with desperation, her unbound hair falling to her shoulders. She was a hostage to despair, appealing to the primitive in man in the pitiful hope of awakening love that might know reverence and respect, I had come upon her suddenly and I was fighting for her in a canyon of crumbling steel against men lost to all honor.

Then I saw the light of the dome that arched above me glowing on her hair and the bright, dangerous, mind's eye vision was gone. I wanted to whisper to her, "A computation denying you the right to marry is a crime against beauty such as yours. Don't accept it. Insist on a more rigorous check on every phase of your ancestry." But I didn't say it. How could a man and a woman reach each other with sympathy and warmth when a terrifying weight of nonhuman wisdom denied them the right to courtship?

A glance is a beginning courtship, a word spoken in a certain way, the briefest of handclasps in a shadowed room. Even that was denied us; we were strangers. There could be no hands stretched forth in friendship and reassurance. If you listened carefully you could hear the humming computers. You could hear the click of the metaltapes being punched, being cut off sharply. You could hear a lifetime of misery and bitter frustration being punched out in exactly ten seconds.

Marriage privilege permitted…Marriage privilege denied.

The vault was like a prison, harsh with artificial sunlight, each of the twenty computation units guarded by heavy bars. You could look up at the glittering tiers of memory banks and stimulus-response circuits, and tell yourself that the Big Brain was society's only bulwark against decay from within. But if the unit before which you stood flashed its cold light upon you, the dryness in your throat wouldn't be from pride.

To the simple fellow yonder, the humming meant that the Big Brain was taking a personal interest in him, as well as every man and woman in the vault, with a solicitude almost godlike. To the junior coordinator whose lips had gone suddenly white, it was quite otherwise. He was an educated man with a high I.Q. and he was waiting for the Giant Computer to make an impersonal analysis of data as unalterable as the stars in their courses.

It was the Giant Computer in the eyes of Society and the technicians who had designed and constructed it. But to the simple fellow and to me, "Big Brain" cut closer to the truth. For quite different emotional reasons perhaps, but what of that? Popular names have a way of demolishing all pretense, and whatever the pros and cons of logic and science, a machine that can destroy your happiness *takes an interest in you.*

Marriage Privilege Permitted...Marriage Privilege Denied.

There is more to it than that, of course. But you had to have good eyesight to read the micro-lettering, which told you exactly why you'd made a tragic mistake in allowing yourself to be born.

Biogenetic advances in electron-microscopic Roentgen-ray analysis having made possible the exact determination of the genes of human inheritance in the human adult, the individual's blindly instinctive urge to mate and have children can now for the first time be successfully controlled. Experience has shown that it is to Society's best interests to maintain at all times a perfect balance of the more desirable genetic types. It thus becomes obvious that curtailment of the marriage privilege must, of necessity, be directed solely to that end.

It was as simple as that. I looked down at my own tape, at the cruel words punched into the metal.

John Tabor...Marriage Privilege Denied.

Ironically, I wasn't an undesirable type. I was perfectly healthy mentally and physically. In a few years—fifteen perhaps—my type could marry again. But right at the moment there were too many of *me.*

If I married now I would be gravely imperiling the beautiful socio-biogenetic balance which had to be preserved—even if it meant enforced celibacy or a freedom ruin for a man who had thought to find his greatest happiness through marriage and a home.

The girl next to me hadn't turned. She was still staring at me and her eyes were clear now—clear and fearless. I hadn't intended to speak to her. I had fought the impulse, knowing what it could lead to. I thought of how vigilantly unlawful lovemaking was spied upon and guarded against, save in the privacy of a man's own lodgings, how every instrument of twenty-second century technology was arrayed against it.

It seldom escaped detection and the penalty—death, or instant, monitor-defying flight to the decadent, violence-ravaged ruins of Nuork. What seemed to some the greater punishment was actually the most merciful, for when survival depends solely on blind luck and a savage, animal-like cunning even the best of men will become brutalized in the end. In Nuork it was kill or be killed and no man could hope to stay alive in a freedom ruin and endure such an exile for more than a year or two. There can be no real freedom in a hunted existence that keeps you constantly on the alert, with violence and death all about you and the dread that you're powerless to cope with it menacing your sanity day and night.

The desires of youth have no beginning, no end. It wasn't sympathy alone that made me ask, "How bad is it?"

"My classical Mendelian ratio is too low," she said. "Too low, that is, for anyone of the pooled offspring of a series of families where the parental mating types are almost identical."

She laughed a little hysterically. "I seem to have memorized it already, word for word. It's strange how you'll do that when everything stops for you and you want to die."

"If it ties in that closely with multiple-family data you can ask for another analysis," I said. "Computations based on more than fifty predictable ratios are sometimes in error."

I showed her my tape. "This is my third computation. I received my first two years ago."

She seemed not to hear me. She was looking at me with suddenly heightened interest, as if my sympathy had brought her new hope and courage. Just my sympathy and not what I'd told her about the multiple family loophole.

She drew closer to me and suddenly there was a flame of yearning between us. I was feeling it and I was pretty sure she was. Her femininity became so overwhelming that it frightened me. I was afraid to think of what might happen if she reached out and touched me. Just the coolness, softness of her palm resting against my arm—

I looked around the vault. A security guard stood by the door, but he wasn't watching us. His eyes were trained on another girl halfway down the vault, a wholly unattractive girl with angular features who stood with her head held high, as if defying the humming computers to deny her happiness.

Spots of color burned in her cheeks and in her eagerness to become a wife and mother she seemed for an instant almost beautiful.

I looked away quickly, feeling I had no right to stare. My temples were throbbing, but I refused to admit that I could be in danger. I had visualized what might happen if she touched me, but I felt confident I could keep that kind of madness at bay. If a woman I did not know was weak and wanted to touch me…I could be strong.

Her hand was suddenly warm in mine, our intertwined fingers shattering my self-assurance and exposing it for what it was—a desperate clutching at a straw.

"Tell me about yourself," she whispered.

Realization came with appalling suddenness. She could have asked anything of me and I could not have refused her. A woman's strength may be different from a man's. But it can be wholly irresistible. There is beguilement in it and subtlety and when the woman is very beautiful a request can be a command.

I told her my name, my occupation, I told her I'd just come from Venus Base and I told her why I was going back. "Hard work is the only real compensation," I said. "When you're engaged in a construction job on the planets you don't have time to think too much. You take pride in your work, in watching the big machines cutting tunnels through solid rock at peak efficiency. You watch the hills being leveled, the sea bottoms being filled in. You watch a city you've helped build rising from firm foundations, white building by white building, and it gives you a feeling of accomplishment. It's better than staying on Earth and seeking a substitute for happiness."

"But is that *real* happiness?" she asked. "Aren't you deceiving yourself?"

"Happiness is always relative," I said. "Life deals every man a few brutal blows, and the happiest men I've known haven't always been the luckiest. It's harder for them when the blows fall."

She nodded in half-agreement, a troubled look in her eyes. As if to dispel thoughts that were painful to her she asked, "What is life on Venus really like, outside of the construction-project sites?"

I told her of the planet's savage beauty, and there was only one thing I kept back—how different I was from most of the men who sought escape on Venus Base. I didn't tell her how great and unusual were my telepathic powers. It was far too dangerous a secret to entrust to a woman. When a child has been born abnormally telepathic he learns caution at an early age—even though he cannot hope to conceal his secret from the Big Brain.

"There are no women on Venus," she whispered.

She was standing very close to me and suddenly her hair brushed my cheek. I told her more about the construction work.

"Men who can't marry on Earth will have their chance," I said. "Women will be sent out. There are restrictions you can't impose on pioneers and builders. The biogenetic heritage requirements won't be quite so strict."

"Women will be sent out when you are dust," she whispered.

I pretended I hadn't heard her. I held on to Venus Base as a child will hold on to its most treasured toy, pretending it has found a way to make it yield adult pleasures.

"The restrictions will be gradually relaxed," I said. "Even now it is a free and easy world. You can travel from construction site to construction site, whenever the desire to roam takes hold of you. To quiet that restless urge women will be sent out. It slows down the entire project. And a new society cannot afford that kind of man-hour waste."

"They will let you die first. The Big Brain has not yet made its power felt on Venus. The monitors know that when men have tasted freedom Society must move with caution." Her fingers tightened on my arm. "Society needs men like you for construction work on Mars and Venus, but those who come after you will be a more docile breed. Society will never reward men whom it does not completely trust."

"I'll have to risk that," I said.

She gave me an odd look. "I suppose it *is* better than sitting under a psycho-helmet dreaming about a woman who exists only in your mind."

"Emotional illusion therapy can be a satisfying experience," I said. "You can have beautiful experiences in dreams. Sometimes it's so real you never want to wake up. The sleeping mind can be aroused and respond to tactile sensations that are memory-recalled without any actual—"

I stopped abruptly, because I wasn't sure it was wise to take her clinical detachment for granted, even on a purely scientific plane. So much depends on the individual's capacity to keep a discussion of the physical aspects of sex compartmentalized. It could take on an emotional coloration that will make what is being said seem outrageously candid and intimate, when nothing could be further from the truth. I had that capacity but the instant I saw a slight flush suffuse her face I hesitated to go on.

She seemed aware of my embarrassment, for she said quickly, "It can be satisfying, I've been told, to a man. But when you *do* wake up?"

"I went to Venus Base because I preferred to stay awake," I said. "Does that answer you?"

Her eyes searched my face. "Did you ever go to a freedom ruin?"

I shook my head.

I would have gone to the freedom ruins, if the stakes had been clear-cut. To be permanently banished to Nuork or one of the other ruins would have been worse, by all counts, than a death sentence. But I would have gone to one for an hour—or a day.

If the stakes had been clear-cut. The women who went expected to be fought over and the men—

You found a woman you could love and you courted her until tenderness and desire flamed in her eyes. Then, unless you were completely a beast, she became your woman for as long as you could hold her. To hold her you would have to kill, to defend and protect her against attack. Not all of the men who went to the ruins in search of a woman were brutes. But they were desperate and despairing men, driven half out of their minds by a hunger the ruins alone could satisfy.

They knew exactly what the stakes were—that it was kill or be killed. And that alone can demoralize a man and make him accept a jungle code. If we are willing to take so great a risk, they told themselves, we have a right to do what every man who comes here must do to stay alive.

It was false and vicious reasoning, because to take a woman by force, even if you are prepared to fight to the death to guard her from further harm, is always a brutal act. And that's why the stakes weren't clear-cut and I had always shunned the ruins. It was possible for a man to go to the ruins and court a woman honorably and openly and win her love. But few of the women who went to the ruins, in a desperate search for a mate, expected to be wooed in that way. They accepted the inevitable and were prepared to submit to violence. Any other kind of lovemaking would have seemed strange to them and by the same token, suspect. They would not have completely trusted a man who wooed them with tenderness and respect.

No society can exist without its safety valves. By computation a certain percentage of the cruelly denied would find their way to the ruins, just as, far back in the twentieth century, a certain percentage of men would seek out women who made a profession of the merchandizing of sex.

A certain percentage would find their way to the ruins and—a certain percentage would die. In that respect it *was* clear-cut.

I could almost hear the Big Brain whispering, "Society has taken certain regions and about them it has erected barriers of self-loathing and public disgrace. Beyond the barriers there is no law but the law of the jungle. Beyond the barriers my wisdom has no meaning. But it is well that some should go; it is necessary."

If the stakes had been just a choice between living and dying I'd have accepted them gladly. But in the ruins men outnumbered women five to one and that gave brutality too large a domain, and generosity and forbearance less than a fool's acre of breathing space. A man could not stand upright in so small a space, and still think of himself as a man.

The eyes of the girl at my side burned into mine. Large eyes she had, a deep, lustrous violet, which looked almost black until you discovered that they could glow for you alone. "Do you know why women who can never have love here go to the ruins?

"This is why!" she said. Her arms went around my shoulder and she crushed her lips to mine, so hard I couldn't breathe for an instant. Then she stepped back quickly, her eyes shining. "Call it anything you wish."

"There's a name for it you don't often hear in the ruins," I said.

She came into my arms again and that was when I brought my mouth down hard on hers; bruising her lips a little and then draining their sweetness like a thirsty wayfarer in a parched wilderness. It was a madness we couldn't control and there was a terrible danger in it.

CHAPTER TWO

WE WERE SAVED from disaster by the totally unexpected.

Far down the vault a man was screaming. His fists were tightly clenched and he was screaming out imprecations against the humming computers. There was a hopeless rage in his eyes—rage and bitter, savage defiance. Even as he screamed he began to slouch forward, with the terrible weariness of a man trapped beyond all hope of rescue.

I had no right to interfere. It was a problem for the Security Guard. The Guard was just starting to turn, the electro-sap at his wrist glittering in the harsh light.

The thought of what might happen made me almost physically ill. I had no right to interfere, but I did, I crossed the vault in six long strides, and grasped the sagging man by the shoulder. I swung him about and started slapping his face. First his right cheek, then his left. It may have been bad psychology, but I had to chance it. I'd seen men killed or crippled for life by electro-saps. Few of the guards were deliberately brutal, but they didn't known their own strength.

Between slaps I spoke to the poor devil in a whisper, deliberately keeping my voice low, knowing that you can't reason with a sick or mortally terrified man by shouting at him.

"Careful—the guard's watching you!" I warned. "Don't force him to use his sap. Do you hear? If you do you won't walk out of here alive!"

Abruptly the poor devil stopped screaming, sagged forward, and would have collapsed if I hadn't caught him.

The guard was instantly at my side. "That was quick thinking, friend. Maybe just a little too quick. Don't you know that helping the wrong people can get you into serious trouble?"

I didn't answer. I just waited, hoping he'd let my interference pass.

He glared at me, then said, "All right, I suppose you can't be blamed too much. I might have done the same thing myself, if it wasn't my duty to see that things stay normal here. When anyone goes off the beam like that, you let him alone for a minute. He may do or say something the Monitors should know about."

He shrugged and most of the animosity went out of his stare. "Get his arm around my shoulder, I want to find out if he can walk."

I stood watching the guard assisting the poor devil out of the vault.

It's funny how tension can distort reality by blocking out what may concern you most by channeling your awareness in just one direction. I watched the guard pass from the vault before I turned back to reassure the girl I'd taken so impetuously into my arms.

She was gone.

For a moment I stood staring around the vault, shaken, despairing. Then, slowly, balance and sanity returned to my mind. I remembered what I'd told her about the mad impulse that had come upon us both at the same time. "Call it anything you wish," she'd said and I'd replied, "There's a name for it you don't often hear in the ruins."

But had I really meant that we'd fallen in love? In ten or fifteen minutes, when we'd been complete strangers to start with? Could love spring up between a man and a woman that fast? Had it ever been known to happen, actually? It's the most precious thing in the world, but all really precious things have a growth stage before they become precious to you. You look at a beautiful emerald and right off it dazzles you, sure. But unless you're as mercenary as hell that emerald doesn't become really precious to you until you've had it set in a ring and worn it for a week or two.

At least a week. You have to turn it about on your finger and hold it up to the light and admire the way it catches and holds the light and delight in the brilliance and splendor of it. It has to become *your* emerald, different from all other precious gems. It must, in a sense, grow into your flesh and sing in your blood and become completely a part of you.

Infatuation? Of course. That could be a singing flame, too and so overwhelming at times it could easily be mistaken for love. It was perhaps the beginning of love—the very first warning you get that you're headed for trouble or an eternity of rapture. Infatuation was seldom wholly physical. Sex entered into it, sure—maybe it was four-fifths sex. But it went much deeper than sex, because you can be physically stirred by a woman and not feel that you're in the slightest danger of becoming really involved with her. Infatuation is sex with something very important added that makes it just about as unique as love, though not as precious to lead at times to a mans total enslavement.

All that I told myself as I stood there completely alone again, realizing with a shudder of relief by what a narrow margin I'd been saved from utter disaster. Unlike the screaming man, I could face the future with confidence.

I was a potential "marriage privilege permitted" type and I knew that hopes temporarily dashed wouldn't stay buried. I knew that when I left the vault and emerged into the clear, bright sunlight it would light up the world for me.

My heart was singing when I turned, and walked out into the corridor and descended to the street.

I wouldn't be lonely any more! She'd be slender and very beautiful, with tumbled, red-gold hair; and when she came forward to greet me for the first time her smile would warm me as I'd never been warmed before.

I had spoken to the man and it was all arranged. I was on my way to pick her up. My beetle purred as it sped swiftly down the shop level driveway, red sunlight gleaming on its fused tungsten hood. The air was crisp, cool and invigorating and the future looked bright.

All I had to do now was conquer a tendency toward fuzzy thinking and face up to the facts. It was as if I could hear the computers humming, giving it to me straight. All right, the computers couldn't talk. You fed them your identity data and the answers came out punched into a metaltape. But it was as if I could hear the Big Brain itself whispering to me.

"Not for you a quiet fireside and a cloak around your shoulders when you're too old to dream, boy! You'll die on Venus Base. You'll be with the lost and forgotten men—or so everyone will think on Earth. But you won't be lost and you won't be forgotten, if you take your happiness while you can. It's yours for the taking, in full measure and brimming over.

"Make the best of things as they are. You've got strength and you've got courage far beyond the average—so take it in your stride. This is the year 2263! There are gadgets, a million satisfying gadgets—glittering and beautiful and new. Gadgets to make up for everything nature or Society or the perversity of fate has denied you.

"There are compensations for every bitter frustration, every handicap of body and mind, every tragic lack of the raw materials of happiness. Men infinitely more unfortunate than you have found substitute satisfactions for everything they've been cheated out of in life. So wade in and wise up. Take a substitute for what doesn't come naturally.

"Drive down to the shop level arcades and buy yourself a wig with synthetic nerve roots which will grow into your scalp. Buy yourself a bone ear, a music or art appreciation groove-in, a money-sense illusion, anything you'd care to name.

"You don't have to be reminded that there are some men, who might say, 'There's no substitute for the real thing. You'll never get around it and you may as well stop lying to yourself.'

"But not you, boy! You'd never say that because you don't give up as easily as that. Naturally they've been keeping it quiet. You have to dial the right shop. You've got to speak in a persuasive whisper to the right people. You've got to mention just how many trips you've made to Venus Base.

"*Buy yourself a beautiful android woman.* Naturally it's labeled: *For Spacemen Only!* If you've got something new and tremendous to sell you'd be crazy to offer it on the open market, wouldn't you? Mass production takes years to build up. Until the mass production stage is reached high profits can only be made without State Bureau interference.

"Why not sell your products to men whose need is so great and urgent—they'll pay specialty prices, in an under-the-counter deal. Pay eagerly and disappear into space.

"It's the only policy that makes sense and you've no quarrel with it, have you, boy? You've spoken to the man and you know exactly what you want and you've the money to pay for it."

The Big Brain, of course, wouldn't speak quite so frankly. It wouldn't conspire with an outlaw firm to deceive the State Bureaus, much as it might want me to accept a substitute for the wife I couldn't have.

I was really listening to a separate, rebellious part of myself arguing with my more cautious self. My reckless self was now completely in the saddle, and I had no real fear that it would come a-cropper. But arguments do no harm and it pleased me to listen to that inner voice hammering home the facts, garnished up a bit by the Big Brain's authority.

We'd better get it straight right at the start that artificial women are as old as the human race. There are Aurignacian Venuses from rock caverns in the Pyrenees you could date in your dreams with no effort at all. Big-bosomed women with flaring hips—the kind of women that Rubens painted and that some men prefer for variety's sake even today. Distinctly on the plump side, but what of that?

What is a statue, really? Hasn't a statue a definite mechanical function to perform? Isn't the statue of a beautiful woman a kind of android designed to delight the eye and trigger the sex mechanism in the human brain? No—perhaps not always designed for that purpose. But doesn't it do that most of the time? Can a normal male pass a shop window and see a beautiful wax mannequin without experiencing at least a faint stirring of sex awareness, even though he knows that a wax woman is quite different from a woman who can think and feel and is in all respects alive?

Consider it honestly. Has it ever failed to happen to you? There's nothing abnormal or perverse about it. The female form, even when it's just a wax replica of the real thing, can do that to the male.

Remember, a statue doesn't have to move at all to be functional in that respect. If a certain arrangement of synthetic lines and curves and dimples can evoke a response in the viewer you've got a mechanical prime mover and if that object happens to be a statue you've got an android in a strict sense. You can even do without the electronic stimulus-response circuits and the Cybernetic memory banks.

The Pygmalion fantasy is the key. Every man carries about with him a subconscious image of the one perfect woman. There's a biological norm and that norm constitutes the ultimate in desirability. Every individual woman departs from the norm to a greater or lesser degree. Nature is constantly attempting to alter the course of evolution through mutational and environmental departures from the norm—mutation plus natural and sexual selection—and that tendency toward variation keeps modifying the norm, throwing it off center.

Features too large or too small will distort or completely shatter the norm. A woman with a too large mouth, for instance, may have other features so perfect that she will still be beautiful. But her beauty won't be perfect if a single one of her features departs from the norm. The closer women approach the norm in all respects the more beautiful they are by human standards.

It's important to accent the *human*. Complete symmetry of features may have a certain classical beauty all apart from sex, but in the main when we say that a woman is beautiful we simply mean that she seems beautiful to us because her features or her body trigger a sexual response. To a Martian—we know now that there is no life on Mars, but the assumption can still be useful—both men and women may seem completely unbeautiful, scrawny, white, hairless bipeds not particularly well formed. We might feel the same way if we could be completely detached and scientific about it. But sex triggers a biological response which prevents us from realizing, in an emotional way, that the human race might not seem beautiful at all if the veil of glamour which sex casts could be stripped away and we could see ourselves as others see us.

There are other, completely human difficulties and complications. On Earth alone the norm varies, and a woman who seems beautiful to an African bushman may not seem beautiful to you. But that does not mean that she is less beautiful. You've got to go back to your ancestry for the key; you've got to find out precisely the kind of norm your ancestors mated with for hundreds of thousands of years.

You could marry anyone of ten thousand women picked almost at random, and be reasonably happy. But to be perfectly content, you have to have a perfect biogenetic mate.

And now, for the first time, you could get your norm girl. Your biogenetic tape recordings supplied the key. You gave the man your biogenetic tape number, all the data available to the Big Brain, and the firm did the rest.

Waiting for me was an android female with a living colloidal brain. The human brain is a colloid with a billion teeming memory cells, made up of molecular aggregates just large enough to be visible in a powerful electron microscope.

Just large enough to be visible. Visibility was the key, for a visible structure can be studied and duplicated. Not exactly, perhaps—we'll get that in another century or so. But enough of the structure could be duplicated to yield results.

I had been warned that there would be no complex emotional overtones in the woman who was awaiting me. A seven-year-old level of intelligence perhaps, no more.

Curiously enough, the limitation did not depress me too much. When physical beauty becomes overwhelming you can think of nothing else. And she would be beautiful, completely my norm girl in her physical attributes. There are many different kinds of women in every man's ancestry, but one kind always predominates and establishes an individual norm preference which corresponds to the ancient tribal preferences of his remote ancestors in a general way. She would undoubtedly resemble quite a few of my great-great-grandmothers.

CHAPTER THREE

THE SHOP LEVEL arcades were a purple and gold glimmer for ten thousand feet. At night the lights are so dazzling that you can't see the individual shop windows, but in broad daylight every window stands out and the level becomes a tunnel of weaving lights and shadows.

It's like plunging into a revolving kaleidoscope to pluck out a rare and glittering prize. Come early, take your pick.

I knew that the shop where I'd left my order would be using some kind of false front. But I wasn't prepared for the beauty of the display that filled the window: a terraced garden with a fountain gushing silver spray, a breathtaking Watteau-gambol of fauns and satyrs in a twilight nymph pursuit.

In the window a little square sign read:

Enjoy Yourself Without Breaking the Law
Which shall it be? Ten Minutes of Emotional Illusion
Therapy Or Ten Months of Freud?

For an instant I was tempted to go inside and forget to mention my name. I knew the routine of the illusion therapy shops backward. If the human brain is paralyzed in certain centers and stimulated abnormally in others, you get an illusion that can only be compared to sheet lightning.

When I closed my eyes I was inside the shop, relaxing in the scented darkness. I could feel the incredible lightness of the big, impulse-transmitting helmet resting on my head. I could hear the therapist saying in a cool, soothing voice: "The women whom you are about to meet are incredibly beautiful. Not one woman, but seven. Now if you'll just relax—"

It's a swift, effective way to cure frustration. But when you wake up, the savor of living is dulled for you, just as heavy smoking often dulls the pleasures of the palate. There is no anticipatory thrill in knowing that the dream experience you've just shared with a non-existent woman can be repeated again and again, and is always available. When you emerge from an emotional illusion therapy trance you couldn't care less. I told myself I'd be crazy to pay that kind of penalty when I could have the real thing.

The man was expecting me. He was tall, quiet and soft-spoken; but I never really got a good look at his face.

You know how it is when you whisper over a wire. Someone has to be at the other end to take down your message. He may be young or old, an executive of the firm or just a front man, a go-between. Instinctively you're almost sure you're not going to like him. When you actually meet him, you see no reason for studying him closely. If he has authority to conclude the deal and wrap it up for you you simply accept him as a vital link in the arrangement. He becomes a person with no real identity, a figurehead. He becomes—the man.

He looked me over carefully. It takes skilled training and insight to judge a man's occupation at a glance. Often as not it's a hit-or-miss task—but if you're really good at it there is always a high-salaried undercover job waiting for you.

He was good at it. You spend two years at Venus Base and it shows in your eyes, the way you carry your shoulders when you walk, the very rhythms of your speech. Spend a lifetime hoeing a field in blazing sunlight or pacing the deck of a ship at sea and you'll get deep creases in the back of your neck, crow's feet about your eyes and a leathery texture of skin such as you can't possibly get if you're a sedentary worker under glass.

Two years at Venus Base can't quite do all that to you, but a really good occupation-guesser can tag you every time.

The man said, "I think you'll be satisfied, sir. But you've got to remember that a woman can be made for just one man alone and not quite satisfy him at first glance."

I wasn't sure I liked the way he smiled when he said that— as if he knew a great deal about women himself and was treating the matter as an amusing episode in the course of his philanderings. As if he'd discovered a girl that suited him fine, and was trying to palm off an old flame on the first gullible lad to walk into the trap. Some girl he'd decided not to like for no particular reason.

"I guess you know that caution is our stock-in-trade," he said. "We have to be careful right from the start. You've got to forgive me if I seem a little ill at ease. I'll be frank with you. The work I do here is not entirely to my liking. In some respects it goes against the grain. By natural inclination I am—well, I should have much preferred to be a creative artist, a painter, or a musician or something of the sort. But I guess we all get sidetracked. You're sidetracked in a bad way."

His eyes grew suddenly sympathetic and for a moment I found myself almost liking him.

"I've been married ten years myself," he said. "My wife is a very attractive woman, and very feminine. All woman, you might say. But you'd be amazed how strong-willed she can be at times. Runs me ragged competing with me. Seems to feel she *has* to compete, and that's always infuriating. A wife should cooperate with her husband, not compete—should give him support when he's going over the hurdles.

"What I'm really trying to say is that married life is never smooth sailing. But I wouldn't want to be alone on Venus Base without a woman. That's one thing I don't envy you lads. To have no woman at all in your life—"

He'd have gone right on talking if I hadn't reminded him that I was very eager to complete my purchase and be on my way. There was a hammering at my temples and my heart was pounding like a bass drum. I'm not being melodramatic. It happened to be true and it wasn't in the least surprising. It was a terribly important moment for me, a critical moment, because if she was really my norm woman and all of my expectations were about to be fulfilled I would walk out of the shop a changed man. There would be so bright a future stretching out before me that the whole of my life—my work and my holiday excursions and moments of creative leisure—would take on a new dimension.

He seemed to sense what was passing through my mind, for he stopped being impulsively over-communicative—it's strange how a harassed man will bare the inmost secrets of his life at times to a total stranger—nudged my arm and said, quite simply: "Follow me."

I accompanied him in total silence along a narrow, dimly lighted corridor and down a short flight of stairs to another corridor with three branching offshoots. We turned right, then left, then right again.

The room was huge and blank-walled. It didn't look like a laboratory where a scientific innovation tremendous in its implications had been successfully carried out, and until the lights came on my thoughts were in turmoil. Would she be as beautiful as I had allowed myself to believe?

I could see vague objects towering the shadows. One caught and held my attention. It looked in the gloom like an enormous stationary globe with shining crystal tubes branching off from it. And that did make the room seem a little more like a laboratory.

The lights came on with a startling abruptness, flooding every corner of the room with a dazzling radiance.

She was lying motionless beneath the globe in a transparent tank filled with weaving lights and shadows, her long, unbound hair descending to her shoulders in a tumbled, red-gold mass that caught and held the radiance.

Her eyes were closed, and her pale beautiful face was turned a little sideways.

She was as I had imagined she would be.

In youth's awakening dreams she had smiled and beckoned to me. The magic of her features was a wondrously changing thing, like the flickering of tail candles on a shrine, or the sunglow on strange beaches in the morning of the world.

Had the poet Shelley dreamed of such a woman when he wrote by the blue Mediterranean: "Her steps paved with gold the downward ravine that sloped to the dawn's bright gleam."

I shut my eyes and we were walking together by the sea, her bronzed loveliness etched against the dawn glow, a miracle Time itself could not tarnish.

I opened my eyes, but for a moment the room seemed remote, unreal. Only the woman in the tank existed for me. She wore a simple white garment, belted at the waist. Her arms and shoulders were bare and her skin had the ruddy glow of perfect health—the natural bronze, which only a warm tropical sun can impart to the skin of northern women who have long embraced its warmth.

Her cheeks were shadowed by long, dark lashes and her mouth was a curving rosebud, and beneath the smooth-textured cloth of her belted tunic her young breasts rose firmly, twin bright mounds in a sea of billowy whiteness.

The sound was faint at first, a barely audible hum. I didn't know it was an alarm for a moment. It sounded more like the drowsy murmur of bees in a noonday glade. But swiftly it grew in volume, turning into a steady and much louder drone, filling me with a sudden uneasiness.

The man turned abruptly and gripped my arm. "It's a Security Police raid!" he whispered, alarm in his eyes. "We've got to get her out of here and upstairs fast!"

I stared at him in consternation. "But why should they raid this shop? Do they know about her?"

He shook his head, his lips white. "Of course not. If the big secret leaked out we wouldn't have just a police raid to worry about. We'd be smashed in a large-scale operation. It's not that at all. There happens to be a law against concealment in an emotional therapy shop—any kind of concealment. We're not supposed to have underground rooms, unless we can prove they're just used for storage purposes."

I'd forgotten about that. Emotional illusion therapy can break down all barriers and lead to actual physical orgies. When men and women are undergoing therapy together the trance will sometimes become a twilight zone between sleeping and waking and they'll behave as they would if they were freedom-ruin outcasts, but with no deep awareness of danger to keep them from going too far. A somnolent state can make even a strong-willed man abandon all restraint, and become the victim of his own inability to distinguish reality from illusion. Even the therapists had at times been overcome and brutally slain, and that danger was always present. It didn't happen often, but the Security Police had to keep a careful check.

"We've got to get her up upstairs," the man insisted, his fingers biting into my arm. "We've got to convince the police there's nothing wrong. She's simply your wife, understand? *She came to this shop with you for therapy.*"

I looked at him, aghast. It didn't make too much sense to me, because married couples seldom needed emotional illusion therapy and if they did they seldom went to the same shop together.

It couldn't be completely ruled out, however, and in that kind of emergency you seize on whatever comes to mind that can give you a fighting chance of getting at least a toehold on firm ground, where skillful lying can do you some good. He'd thought fast, and it dawned on me that he could have panicked and done just the opposite and I was grateful to him for not letting go. But that didn't mean I wasn't torn by doubts.

"She hasn't said a word to me!" I protested. "She's lying there in a deep sleep. She *is* asleep, isn't she? Speak up, man! What do you want me to do?"

"I'll wake her up," he said. "I'm going to attach an electric stimulator to her right temple and wake her up right now. Then you've got to help me lift her out of the tank. We haven't a moment to lose!"

He did exactly what he said he'd do. I watched him, a dull pounding at my temples, resenting the fact that she could not awaken to me alone. For a few tormenting seconds I forgot the danger we were in and the presence of an outsider seemed like a desecration. He'd become an outsider the instant I'd set eyes on her, and I regretted that she could not awaken to me in a moonlit garden in the first bright flush of dawn.

We had no chance at all to be alone, for the instant she opened her eyes, he removed the electric stimulator from her brow and turned to me in urgent appeal.

"Come on, we've got to hurry," he urged. "Help me lift her out. She isn't heavy."

I had an impulse to knock him down. If there was any lifting to be done I wanted to do it alone. Then I remembered that you can't walk into a shop and make a purchase of any kind without assistance.

In another twenty minutes, if the police could be outwitted, the man would be an ugly, receding memory— nothing more.

Another thought struck me, incredible at such a time. I hadn't even asked her name. "I don't know her name," I heard myself saying, my voice suddenly out of control. "Tell me her name—then I'll help you."

He seemed startled and taken aback by my sudden vehemence. "You can give her any name that suits your fancy."

He lost his temper then, for the first time. "Do you want me to give you a catalogue of women's names? Gloria, Anne, Helen—the face that launched a thousand ships—Barbara, Janice—pick one quickly and let's get on with this."

His features hardened. "The Security Police won't be interested in your romantic ideas. They'll put you through a grilling. You'll have to know something about her, not just her name alone."

The shock of the sudden raid must have thrown me off my rocker. But I didn't feel like apologizing to him. I still felt that she should have a name.

I knew that if I named her under pressure I might regret it later. But I had no choice. *Claire* I thought. *Claire will do for now.*

I stepped quickly to the man's side and together we lifted Claire out of the tank, and set her on her feet.

In the tank with her eyes closed her beauty had seemed breathtaking. But the instant she was on her feet, facing me, the instant she opened her eyes and looked straight at me I couldn't speak at all.

"Say something to her!" the man urged. "You've got to get acquainted fast. Speak up—she'll answer you!"

I cleared my throat, "I'm John, Claire," I said. "Look at me, Claire. Don't be afraid."

She had never seen me before, of course. But I knew that an artificial memory picture of my general aspect had been skillfully stippled into her mind. A colloidal memory-chain implant that would be activated when she saw me standing before her.

Her voice was low and musical and it matched in all respects the wondrous beauty of her features. "John," Claire said. "John, *John.*"

I knew that a bond of sympathy and understanding could only be established between us if I talked to her at first about simple things—the few simple things a man and a woman meeting for the first time and sharing certain basic memory patterns, would have in common.

"Yes, I'm John, Claire," I reiterated. "Do you like me?"

She stared at me as if puzzled. "I like you," she said.

My heart skipped a beat. I leaned forward and put my arm about her shoulder. "I am taking you away with me, Claire," I told her. "You have never seen the city with your own eyes. There are memories of the city in your mind, but they are not living memories. You will like the city, Claire."

"I will like the city."

I took her hand. It was warm and soft and the fingers closed quickly on mine.

A torturing doubt had crept into my mind. So far her words had done little more than parrot my own. I had dangled a promise before her, had opened a gate on shining adventure that would have delighted a child. Would not a child have asked, "Will it be fun?" or "Have you a beetle? Will we go riding?"

The man was becoming impatient. "We've got to hurry," he warned. "If the police find this room I can't answer for the consequences. They're probably checking everything over upstairs and that takes a little time. With no one in the shop, they'll be doubly suspicious if they have the slightest reason to suspect there's someone down here. Our luck has held so far. But don't press it."

He looked steadily at me. "You've put her at ease. She's not as startled as I was afraid she might be. Be satisfied with that, can't you? Do you have to make love to her?"

His eyes flashed angrily when I didn't say a word. "We made her especially for you and you're not satisfied," he complained. "You have to start playing all the stops immediately. You wouldn't do that with a new musical instrument. You'd have more sense."

He had a point there, all right. But how wise had been my decision not to study him too closely. I knew that the memory of that moment would always hold emotional overtones of ugliness for me. It would always make the illusion a little less than perfect, a sordid reminder that he *could* compare her to a musical instrument, and that I hadn't met her in a moonlit garden at the home of an old and trusted friend.

He had nothing further to say and neither did I, I followed his advice and together we walked Claire out of the room, and along a corridor thronged with flickering shadows and up a narrow flight of stairs to the shop.

THERE WERE TWO police officers waiting for us in the shop, close to the big metal helmets which gave the customers the kind of illusions that could shut out the Law completely.

For us the policemen were real and they were earnest.

The instant they saw us they did a slow double take. One was burly with muscular shoulders and a florid, granite-firm jaw. The other was a skinny bantamweight.

The burly one did all of the talking. The instant he saw us he asked, "You two together?"

The man answered for me. "Mr. Tabor is one of my regular customers," he said, quickly. "This is his wife."

The officer planted his hands on his hips and looked Claire up and down. "Married folk, eh? Did you put on the helmets together?"

I knew that I had to think fast. The question was a deliberately insulting one, obviously designed to trap us.

"I just dropped in to make an appointment for next week," I said. "Mrs. Tabor doesn't take emotional illusion therapy."

The officer grinned. "No repressions, eh?"

If Claire had really been my wife the question would have infuriated me, I became angry anyway. The officer saw the flushed look come into my face and it aroused his suspicions.

He moved closer to Claire and studied her face. "Been married long?"

Claire shook her head. Such reticence wasn't natural in a woman confronted with that kind of smirking impertinence and I could see that the officer felt that he was making progress.

"I shouldn't think your husband would need emotional illusion therapy if you've just been married," he said. "I'm curious to know exactly how long you've been married. Seven months? A year?"

Claire didn't say a word.   If she'd looked deeply bewildered or too angry to speak it might have helped.   But there was just a look of awakening interest in her eyes, as if she couldn't quite decide what the officer was talking about, but was doing her best to fit him into a new-impression category in her mind.

A very young child has to make such an effort constantly, for his experience is too limited to enable him to grasp the implications of the many startling things that keep taking place around him.   He just isn't aware of how ugly and threatening life can be at times.   Not until he burns his fingers and learns the painful way.   And by then it's frequently too late.

"It's none of my business, I suppose," the officer said. "But it does make a difference.   If you were married recently your husband shouldn't need emotional illusion therapy at all. It goes without saying that the woman a man marries may turn out to be the really cold kind.   He can't always be sure in advance.   You *could* be that way, but—well, if you were my wife just your looks alone would keep me out of an illusion therapy shop for at least five years."

It was envy, mixed with admiration that was making him talk that way.   He was the blunt, coarse type and that kind of man has to have some aggressive outlet for his frustration when authority goes to his head.   I knew all that and perhaps I should have accepted it as inevitable, and kept my anger bottled up until he went too far and forced me to resort to violence.   But you can't think realistically when rage makes you want to grab him by the shoulders and bang him around until he flattens out on the floor.

I might even have killed him, because something very primitive in me was ripping my self-control to shreds. An affront to yourself alone is one thing. You can sometimes exercise control when you know that the whole weight of Society can be hurled against you if you don't, no matter how unjustly. No man can hope to buck that kind of power. But when the affront is directed against a woman who has the innocence of a child and no way of parrying it, a woman who has suddenly become far more precious to you than your own life—

He went on as if he wasn't even aware of the danger he was in. "It's an important thing to get straight. In fact, there are laws against illusion therapy for the newly married, unless the head shrinkers decide there's some very drastic need for it. There's a waiting list for cases like that, a lot of papers to sign. Otherwise thousands of honeymooners would crowd in when there's no real need for them to compensate for anything. People are like that. You make a fad out of something and everyone has to try it at least once."

A cynical smirk twisted his lips. "Sex is like everything else—you feel you can never get too much of it, even when you know it makes no sense. Give a man a big, expensive dinner with all the trimmings, and tell him that there's another one waiting to be served to him, with a different kind of main dish, and he'll forget that he won't be that hungry when he's through gorging himself. Especially if you tell him that everyone's doing it. Two big dinners every night—a popular fad. You have to prove you're as good as the next man at it, or you think you do. And Society suffers in the end."

Out of the mouths of babes a little wisdom sometimes comes and it's just as true with the blunt, crudely outspoken types. Purely by accident a man like that can hit the nail so squarely on the head that you have to admire him a little, if only because there is more than a trace of forthright bluntness in all of us that is wholly on the coarse side. It's one way of giving that part of yourself a pat on the back.

But right at the moment I wasn't even thinking of that. If I'd given him a pat it would have hurled him back against the wall and turned him into a stretcher case.

He narrowed his eyes and looked at Claire even more steadily. "Now suppose you answer my question. Just how long have you two been married?"

Claire said, "John is my husband, I like John. John likes me."

That did it. The officer swung on me, the veins on his temples pulsing like seaworms on a mud flat when the tide is running out.

"Can't she answer simple questions?" he demanded. "What is she—a moron?"

"Now wait a minute—" I choked.

He didn't give me a chance to lunge at him. He beckoned to Skin-and-Bones and the little bantamweight grabbed my arm from behind. I was caught so completely off-guard that I thought for an instant that a muscular spasm had jerked the bones of my wrists right out of their sockets. Skin-and-Bones' fingers seemed to have the tensile strength of steel.

"We'll have to take you both in for questioning," the burly officer said. "She must have something to conceal, or she'd speak up."

There was a shark-toothed rasp to his voice that made me think of the sea again, probably because there's a cold, cruel rapacity about the sea that even its great surface beauty can't hide.

There was nothing beautiful about the burly officer, on the surface or otherwise.

"She must have something to conceal," he reiterated, "or she wouldn't try to make me think she has no brains at all."

I went completely berserk then. I straightened my shoulders, wrenched my wrists free despite the bantamweight's eight-ply grip and gave him a violent shove. Skin-and-Bones gave a startled gasp, as if it had never happened to him before. Without turning, I grabbed Claire by the wrist, and we started for the door.

Instantly the burly cop stepped in front of us and barred our path. "Now you're really in trouble. You've attacked an officer in the performance of his duty."

There was only one thing to do. I took a slow step backward and sent my right fist crashing against his jaw. I put all of my strength into the blow, counting on the advantage of surprise. I followed through with a hard left to the stomach, the kind of jab that had served me well on Venus Base on a good many occasions.

He let out a yell, staggered back and collapsed against the wall. Sinking to the floor with a grotesque swaying of his entire bulk.

I gripped Claire's wrist again. "Trust me and don't look back," I whispered urgently. "We've got to keep moving!"

We were out of the shop before the big officer could flatten out on the floor. We ran swiftly across the pavement outside and climbed into my beetle, I ascended first and helped her straddle the safety rail and settle down at my side, keeping a tight hold on her arm.

"You made him sit down!" she gasped.

"For a minute," I said. "He'll be on his feet again before we've gone three miles. I took the bark out of him, but not the bite. When he gets up a general alarm will go out and we'll be in the deadliest kind of danger."

"Danger?" she breathed. "We will be—in *danger?*"

When you're under great tension in the presence of a child and feel you must talk you're likely to say what's on your mind even if you know you can't count on adult understanding. You're really half talking to yourself and don't expect an adult response.

I didn't get one, but what she *had* said surprised me, because it was a big leap forward. For the first time she hadn't just parroted my words. She had spoken with a rising inflection, had asked me a direct question. For the first time there was strong emotion in her voice. It may or may not have been fear but I was pretty sure that the word "danger" had puzzled and alarmed her.

Swiftly the beetle picked up speed, sweeping up the driveway with a dull roar.

I looked at Claire, sitting straight and still at my side, and felt a fierce surge of exaltation. I'd broken the law for a beautiful woman for the first time in my life.

We were getting acquainted fast.

Perhaps it was the heady wine of an exhilaration that was completely new to me which made me reckless. At any rate, I said something to her I had wanted to say in the shop, in defiance of the man's presence.

"Claire," I whispered.

She looked at me as if startled. "Claire is my name."

"I know," I said. "You just said you liked me. Could you say, 'I love you'?"

"I love you," Claire said. Her voice was strangely toneless, automatic.

"Say it again," I urged.

"I love you," Claire said.

There it was, but it just didn't mean anything to her. I could tell by the way she said it.

Would it mean anything later? Would she ever say, "John, my dearest one, I will love you until I die? Night and day you are never absent from my thoughts."

Whether the miracle would ever take place, right at the moment I knew I'd have to think and move fast and put every other consideration aside.

When a general alarm goes out every traffic tower becomes a scanning trap. With luck you can sometimes outwit a Security Police network, on the human level. The law isn't infallible and never has been. But when invisible beams fasten on you and start working you over, the odds against you really start mounting.

Put a frog in a glass of water—any ordinary bullfrog mottled green and brown—and it will start shedding skin cells at a prodigious rate. No two frogs are ever exactly alike and a frog in a glass would have little chance of keeping its identity a secret from a determined research biologist.

We were in the same kind of trap. I knew that before we could travel a mile after the alarm went out, identity-ray projectors would scan my skin, hair and optic disks. They would scan me from head to toe, with scant regard for my modesty. They wouldn't miss a square inch, and the whorl-findings would be flashed to Central Identification; and at Central my name disk would slide from the big general file, and go clicking into an emergency alert slot.

They'd have me tabbed in almost nothing flat.

I reached over and gripped Claire's arm. "When we get out—keep close to me," I warned. "Do you understand? Close, right at my side. We've got to make a dash for it."

To make sure that my advice would be followed and remain clear in her mind I acted it out in pantomime the instant we were on the pavement. I took five swift steps forward, returned to her side and advanced again, making it plain that she should try to match her steps with mine and not let the distance between us widen by more than a yard.

She seemed to catch on. I'd halted the beetle in the middle of the block, flush with the curb, after making sure that an old subway entrance was less than sixty feet away.

I knew we'd have to reach it fast. As we turned from the car a siren started screaming, and out of the corner of my eye I could see that an orange-colored police beetle was heading straight for us at a distance of perhaps two hundred feet.

I hadn't driven the car right up to the subway entrance because there was a weed-choked, debris-cluttered lot on the street side and the only way to get to it was on foot. The lot said as plain as words: "This is where it begins—the decay of order and public safety. This is where degradation begins. Society does not choose to beautify what it can barely endure. Let the rust and neglect and the slow crumbling serve as a warning, a symbol of what this portal stands for. To enter it is to be self-condemned and bear a burden of guilt which will grow heavier hour by hour, day by day—until death decides the issue in a freedom ruin for a man cut off from all hope."

For half a century no subway entrance had been cleared of rubble. They were ugly defacements in the midst of whitely gleaming streets and tree-lined squares. But the weight of a firmly established tradition can override Man's dislike of ugliness and turn an entire society schizoid by giving it a blind spot.

I was sure that Claire did not know what "schizoid" meant. It was not necessary for her to know. Only that the danger had become so acute that our lives hung in the balance, I reached for her hand and we started off.

"Don't look back!" I warned.

Surprisingly, Claire was good at running. She ran swiftly at my side, her feet clattering on the hard pavement. I let go of her hand almost immediately, for I had merely grasped it to give her reassurance. The siren sound rose higher, became a steady, terrifying drone.

Halfway down the block three Security Police officers in uniform descended from a careening beetle, and raced toward us, letting the car plunge on under automatic controls.

It was then that Claire made her first serious mistake.

My advice must have made a deep impression on her, for she kept close to me as she ran—too close. Thinking she was at least two feet from me I swerved sharply and collided with her, hurling her violently back against a traffic guidepost.

The post was magnetically energized, and it caught and held her firmly. It startled and frightened me. I grasped her by both shoulders and stared at her in alarm. "Hold perfectly still," I cautioned. "One wrench will free you, but you mustn't move."

Obviously there was a band of metal under her dress.

It shocked me to realize that I hadn't even had time to ask the man about that. Just how much metal had been used to manufacture Claire?

When I had helped the man lift her from the tank her body had seemed soft and yielding enough. But just how much metal had been used? A band less than four inches wide would have held her fast to a magnetized traffic post. But what if Claire was more of an artificial woman than I had dreamed?

It was the worst possible time to have such thoughts.

It was also the best time, because the danger we were in prevented me from tormenting myself by letting my mind run in that direction for longer than a second or two.

I told myself that metal magnetized to only a moderate extent wouldn't hold fast if I gave it a really violent wrench.

I exerted all my strength and Claire swung clear.

As she lurched forward into my arms one of the pursuing officers opened fire on us. The bullet went wild, splintering the traffic post at its base. I grabbed Claire's wrist and we started running again.

She was still good at it. It seemed only an instant before we reached the subway entrance and were swept into its dark, protective embrace.

As the clamor from outside fell away our feet set up a hollow echoing that resounded through the darkness until even the terrifying siren wail dwindled to a far-off, ghostly mockery of sound.

Then we stopped to regain our breath, and Claire swayed toward me. I caught her in my arms and held her tightly, whispering words of reassurance to her until her trembling ceased.

I hadn't intended to kiss her. It wasn't the right moment for that, but there was no way I could have controlled the impulse, for it sprang from a threefold need. I had to know if her lips would part as the lips of the girl in the vault had done and yield an even greater sweetness. I had to be sure that they were as warm and alive and vibrant as they would have to be if I wanted to kiss her again and again, tomorrow and the next day and for as long as we were together with all of my doubts swept away... And I had to make certain that I would be glad that we had been lovers if I had only that to remember, if disaster overtook us before we could experience the whole of love's rapture and surrender ourselves to long hours of just being alone together in the silence of the Venusian night, with a wilderness of stars overhead and only night-flying birds to spy on us.

She gave a strange little cry when I brought my lips down on hers, not hard or crushingly, for I did not want to frighten her, but so gently that I felt almost foolish and ill at ease for a moment. Can lovemaking ever fail to be impetuous and still transport you into another world, full of light and fire? Can you make love passionately without hardly seeming to do so, keeping your arms resting lightly on a woman's shoulders, and not even venturing to caress her hair?

I would not have thought so until her lips melted into mine and the gentlest of kisses became so prolonged, sweet and intimate a miracle that I could have asked for nothing more. I was content with the kiss alone.

Once or twice in my life I have experienced the wonder of such a kiss in my dreams. A girl in the first flush of young womanhood, fragile and lovely beyond belief, can kiss you that way in a dream and when you wake up you're glad you didn't let yourself go, because complete physical intimacy would have somehow marred the perfection of an experience so unforgettable.

Cynics may sneer and far back in the twentieth century an orthodox Freudian would have been quite confident that he knew exactly how to interpret that kind of dream. But he would have been wrong. It wasn't dividing sex into two categories and only letting yourself go with the really wanton kind of woman. It wasn't having a fear of letting yourself go with the super-respectable, super-chaste kind. It just wasn't…because that slender, incredibly beautiful girl was sex personified. You could have let yourself go easily enough, with no inhibitions and no restraint. But a kiss alone can be a kind of idealization of love on a super-romantic plane, and can linger hauntingly in your memory for days—all the sweetness and wonder of it. In a way, it *is* complete physical intimacy, if it is passionately sensuous and prolonged…

The very attenuation of the experience seems to make it more intense and hauntingly beautiful, so that you're stirred to the depths. It could stem to some extent from a Western European culture-complex distortion in regard to sex—a Medieval troubadour over-glorification of just the romantic aspects of sex. But that doesn't mean that such an over-glorification isn't basic to human nature everywhere on Earth, only waiting for the right soil, the right historic moment, to take hold of Man's unconscious in an almost compulsive way.

It's basic enough and from whatever source arising, the old Freudians would have been wrong.

"Darling, they would have been wrong!" I said.

I didn't expect her to understand, of course. But when I released her, the way her eyes seemed to be shining made me almost sure that the way I'd felt when the kiss had gone on and on had somehow gotten through to her. She didn't say a word and it was too early to take even that for granted. She could have felt nothing, for her response could have been wholly automatic. She'd been made for me, hadn't she? All of my norm-woman data requirements were on punched tapes, and the firm knew exactly what kind of a romantic fool I could be.

We were still in great danger. Ordinarily the Security Police have no arrows left to their bows when you plunge into a subway entrance and flee toward a freedom ruin. But they have been known to continue the pursuit, if what the Big Brain tells the monitors about you is alarming enough. They have even been known to go right into the ruins after men and women whose defiance has been so outrageous that Society cannot permit them to escape. They do not hesitate to risk their lives against overwhelming odds, if the emergency is grave enough, and the right to be an outcast, guilt-tormented and exposed on every side to brutal violence, can't be countenanced without setting a precedent others might seize upon. A deliberate, willfully planned rebellion could blow the top right off the safety valve provided by the ruins, and the monitors knew it.

CHAPTER FIVE

CLAIRE CONTINUED to keep close to me as we moved forward through the echoing darkness, her face mirroring a strange, new wonder. The blue steel tracks seemed to fascinate her. She kept stopping to stare at them; once she bent and ran her fingers over a gleaming rail, back and forth, as if the coolness of the metal surprised and delighted her.

There was one rail I was careful not to touch, even with my feet, as I ran. It was known as the third rail, and touching it was supposed to bring bad luck; the superstition was as ancient as the tracks themselves.

How it originated nobody knew. Maybe when people rode on the trains centuries ago young daredevils descended into the tunnel and ran recklessly along the third rail until a train came roaring toward them. It would have been a game—wild, reckless and fearfully dangerous—quite as mentally intoxicating as filling the chambers of a primitive hand gun with six bullets, pressing the gun to a vital center, and letting your life or death be decided by a single, quick turn of the revolving cylinder.

How many of the young daredevils had leapt aside in time? How many had died hideously beneath grinding wheels, their bodies crushed and mutilated without reason, primitive victims of the old Freudian "death wish"?

It's curious how the human mind will seize on strange ancient rites and customs in moments of great peril, as if there was something in human nature which made the dangers and follies of the remote past seem an audacious pathway by which modern man could escape to a more primitive level of consciousness. When men lived with their whole bodies, and not just with their minds alone, danger took on an intoxicating, heady quality, which our own age has lost.

"Why do we walk here?" Claire asked.

"Don't be frightened," I said. "We'll come to an exit soon."

Her next question startled me by its childlike innocence, "Will it stay dark?"

"No," I assured her. "We'll go up out of the darkness into light."

I kept looking at her face. She wasn't a child in her beauty, her strange and vibrant warmth. Why did I keep forgetting that I had what few men before me had ever possessed—the rare grace and loveliness of a perfect illusion?

Her perfection was absolute. Could any man with the blood warm in his veins have asked for more? There was something eerily poetic about her speech. She spoke of darkness, light, fire, walking, running, as if each new experience was the personification of some elemental force, much as a child looking up at the new moon might croon with pleasure, and ask to be taken for a ride through the night sky in a chariot of fire.

What right had I to feel disappointed? I told myself that I ought to feel grateful and very humble in the presence of that kind of thinking, imagining.

But what I told myself, and what I wanted with every mad impulse of my heart and brain, were two different things. A man wants to be able to swing an adored woman around impulsively, and whisper: "Darling, remember that tune? Remember the last time we heard it? Remember how funny you looked with your strawberry curls whipped by the wind? Remember how rough the sea looked, with the whitecaps dancing up and down? Remember the fishermen coming in from the beach, and how their nets caught and held the sunlight?

"Remember, darling? Remember, remember? The balcony was just like this one, but you look even more beautiful by moonlight. What are we waiting for? Come on, let's dance!"

She saw it before I did, the light flooding down over the tracks a hundred feet ahead. She gasped with delight, and broke into a run.

I stared at her, startled. It was her first completely impulsive act, breaking away from me like that without a word. Maybe she had a better brain than I had dreamed.

When I caught up with her, she was out of breath from running and my hope leapt high. But then she spoke, and something went dead inside of me. "I did not want the light to go away."

I looked at her. "Is that why you ran so fast—to catch the light?"

She nodded, obviously pleased by my quick understanding. A child mind, poetic and strange.

I stared up at the platform looming darkly through the shadows. Very carefully I measured the distance with my eyes. "I'm going to put my arm around your waist and lift you up," I told her. "Do you understand?"

"No," she said.

I stared at her in dismay. "Well—hold still, anyway," I pleaded.

For the first time I put both my arms around her, and held her tight. I was aware of her breathing, the rise and fall of her bosom.

A line from a half-forgotten poet flashed through my mind: *Man begins by loving love and ends by loving a woman, but a woman begins by loving a man and ends by loving love.*

I told myself angrily that such a thought at such a moment was absurd, and I forced myself to counterbalance it by repeating to myself another line: *Love is a conflict between reflexes and reflections.*

I could feel her trembling as I tightened my hold on her waist. "Up we go!" I whispered.

She wasn't very heavy. It's curious how, when you get started on quotations, you can't easily stop. Another line came to me, urging me to make haste. *Dost thou love life? Then do not squander time, for that is the stuff that life is made of.*

She wasn't heavy, but lifting her to the edge of the platform nearly wrenched my arms from their sockets. The platform was three feet above my head, even when I stood on tiptoe, and Claire let me do all of the hoisting.

I lifted her over the edge and waited until she started crawling away from me on her hands and knees. Then I climbed up beside her and helped her to her feet.

We went up the crumbling stone steps into the sunlight.

For how many generations had the abandoned subway entrances loomed as symbols of escape to a freedom debased and turned into a cruel mockery by a jungle savagery beyond Society's control? Tradition had left them standing for a purpose, surely, for each one led to the same central wasteland of crumbling stone and steel.

When you enter the ruins, with no intention of turning back, resolute of mind and will, the first half-hour is the worst. You're without firm anchorage of any sort. You know that eventually you'll find a place to live, you'll make friends. But until you do your life hangs by a thread.

No man or woman can go it alone in the ruins. You've got to take root fast. You've got to send sturdy roots deep into the strange new soil before a bullet crashes into your spine, or a knife buries itself between your shoulder blades.

I tightened my hold on Claire's hand, and we moved along the ancient streets in complete silence. We walked past rubble-choked intersections, which had once pulsed with light and traffic. The buildings were dark with age, their walls rusted and overgrown with climbing vines. The doors swung idly on their hinges, and there were ominous, blood-hued shadows and sagging signs everywhere.

Bakery. Tilson's Gas Station. Cut Rate Drugs.

So far not even a shadow had crossed our path.

Was the ruin deserted? I'd heard of ruins abandoned in superstitious fear, ruins where women—made desperate by loneliness—had refused to be fought over. They'd done their own choosing, picking one man and killing four, laughing as they discouraged all further pursuit.

Outcast girls were often crack marksmen. I pictured myself crushing such a woman in my arms, a man of her own choosing, crushing her and holding her while I watched the fury and contempt in her eyes turn to an unfamiliar warmth which startled her, and widened her eyes, and brought her lips tight against mine.

There were depths in human psychology I could never hope to fathom.

I saw a door standing half-open, and on impulse kicked it wide. With my arm about Claire's waist, I pushed forward into the shadows.

The music was a wild, frenzied burst of sound. It came from a towering, rainbow-colored shape of metal and glass, which stood against a crumbling wall spattered over with dark stains.

There were several tables standing about, and at one of them sat a girl with jet-black hair, and wide, startled eyes. She was staring straight at me in the gloom.

Quickly my eyes passed over her, lingering on the one-piece, silvery-textured suit, and the bared right leg with the small stocking knife held well in place. There was mud on her ankles, and her shoes were worn down from running on pavements of crumbling stone and gravel like a hunted creature of the night.

"Come in, and shut the door!" she pleaded.

The door seemed to come loose in my hands. It closed with a frightful rasp, and a chink of light came through from outside, spilling across the floor and pointing directly at me like an accusing finger.

I said automatically, "Were you waiting for someone?"

Her eyes bored into mine in a level, challenging stare. "For you."

I recognized her then. She had gone out of my life fast, and returned fast. Only, this time, there was no punched metaltape gleaming on her palm, no Security Guard watching us from the shadows.

Poetry again, a crazy line flashing through my mind. *Her young breasts brightening into sighs.* The fantasy I'd succumbed to in the vault had come true; I could only stare, moisten my lips, and wonder if I had gone quite mad.

I looked at Claire, standing straight and still at my side. She was staring at the outcast girl with friendly interest, as a child might stare at a performing bear in a carnival of animals.

How close can a man feel to two women at the same time? If you hold one in your arms, and she's tender and yielding, and her lips are fire, can you look over her shoulder at another woman with a childlike stare who speaks in monosyllables, and whispers, "You'll never know how much you mean to me, my darling!"

In some ways Claire was closer to me than the girl at the table. I had held her in my arms too; I knew her name—and how could I fail to be stirred by her trust and utter dependency?

Don't be a fool, a voice whispered deep in my mind. *You're drawn to both women. It's as natural as breathing for a man to be drawn to two women—a dozen. It can happen at any time.*

Surprisingly, Claire's hand had crept into mine. Her fingers tightened and relaxed, then tightened again.

I tried to keep my voice calm. "How did you know I was coming here? You couldn't have followed me when I left the vault. I had my own beetle, and I drove fast."

"And looked behind to make sure?" she inquired, mockingly.

She laughed at my sudden alarm.

The police raid *had* puzzled me. Emotional illusion therapy shops are seldom raided before noon. Treatments do not, as a rule, take place in the early hours of the morning, and what herdsman would send beaters across an entire mountainside to capture one goat?

Had she actually followed me from the Giant Computer vault to the therapy shop, and notified the police? The thought seemed incredible; I rejected it, even before she said, "When I left the vault I knew we'd meet again. Your need was as desperate as mine."

Her eyes brightened with a sudden, wild yearning, with a hint of voluptuousness startling in its candor.

"Your need was as desperate as mine, and I knew we'd meet in the ruins, I knew you'd come in search of me, with the memory of my lips burning yours. I knew it would be only a matter of hours until you found me."

Suddenly, she seemed to see Claire for the first time, to realize the significance of Claire. Her eyes narrowed, and her voice became less assured. "You did not come alone," she said. "Where did you find this girl? Who is she?"

"Her name is Claire," I said. "I did not meet her here, and I did not come here in search of you."

Her eyes widened in swift amazement, then narrowed again, fastening on Claire in angry disbelief. She half rose from the table, the quickness of her breathing revealing how deeply she had been hurt.

To appease her I said quickly, "We had some trouble with the police. I could have identified myself and straightened it out, but Claire needed my help desperately. They could have held her on a technical charge, just out of spite. A minor infraction, of no importance, but you know how the police can be when they're envious of another man's interest in a beautiful woman."

"You're interested in her, are you?"

"I've known Claire for a long time," I lied. "She's younger than you'd suspect—just turned eighteen. You ought to realize it's natural enough for a man my age to take a fatherly interest in a second cousin as young and inexperienced as Claire. There's nothing serious between us, if that's what you've been thinking."

"That's exactly what I've been thinking," the girl from the vault said.

For a moment I was afraid that her anger would continue to mount. But after what must have been for her a bad moment, she resumed her original position at the table, making no effort to conceal the shapely grace of her bared right knee.

"That was cattish of me," she said. "Why shouldn't I believe you? You are not the kind of man who would allow himself to be trapped in a lie—even to a woman so foolishly and recklessly emotional that she would hold you quite blameless."

She cast down her eyes suddenly, allowing her fingers to stray for an instant to the securely sheathed stocking knife.

"It is easy enough to say that jealousy is for children. It is easy enough to say that a man or a woman in love should be completely an adult. But we know better—you and I. You have been to Venus Base, and I have been denied a woman's right to happiness."

She raised her eyes and looked directly at Claire, her lips curving in a smile. "Hello, Claire!" she said. "I'm Agnes."

She motioned to a chair. "Sit down, Claire. You look tired."

Claire sat down quietly and folded her hands in her lap. She looked at me, as if to make sure I did not disapprove.

"Tell me about yourself, Claire," Agnes urged. "Just how did you get in trouble with the police?"

I started to intervene, but was stopped by a sudden change in Agnes' expression. Her eyes had widened in alarm; she was leaning sharply forward, gripping the table with both hands.

CHAPTER SIX

I SWUNG about. Three men had entered the tavern and seated themselves at tables near the door. They were surly looking ruffians, heavy of muscle and bone, and they sat watching us with a stillness that was ominous.

The one nearest to me was big—really big. I could see at a glance that he had been in a good many fights, and that each fight had left its mark on him. His nose was badly battered, crooked and flattened at the tip. His ears were misshapen, mere fleshy lobes flattened grotesquely, so that they spread out over his cheeks like crushed cauliflowers. His right cheek was further defaced by a livid scar, and there was something about the scar, which made me see him in another situation—facing three or four men trying with insane rage to cripple him for life.

It was a mind's-eye vision, but it was so vivid I could see the flash of the knife as it grazed his cheek; I could see him backing away without a sound, a faint smile of contempt curling his lips.

He certainly wasn't a very handsome-looking baby, but all of my instincts warned me that what he lacked in looks he could make up for in other ways.

He was staring at Claire. Not at Agnes, but at Claire, with a curious intent look, his eyebrows arched as if in amazement.

His attitude did not surprise me. Girls like Claire were not often seen in the ruins. In the ruins, striking beauty really stood out. Put a flaming orchid in a rock garden overgrown with weeds, and that one solitary bloom will create a world of its own, so dazzling that the wrong kind of man will kill to possess it.

It didn't take Ugly Face long to recover from his surprise. When I saw his eyes leave Claire's face and pass down over her, I had a pretty good idea how long it would take him to whip out a knife.

What I did was the logical outgrowth of what I was—a telepath, a man who could read the mind of an adversary in a moment of deadly danger.

There was one table between us. The instant he started to rise I leapt toward it, gripped it firmly and raised it high. The speed with which I moved seemed to cast a spell upon him. He froze facing me, his hand arrested half way to his hip.

Before the spell could snap I hurled the table straight at him.

This is Ugly Face, and you've hit him with a table smack on the chest! Try it sometime. Shudder to the impact of solid wood cracking against muscle and bone. It will make you want to cry out with the torturing uncertainty of it. Something will tighten inside you, you'll have a wild impulse to follow up the assault with flailing fists, a bellow of rage.

But if you're wise, you won't move in too quickly.

The table spun Ugly Face around, sent him staggering back against the wall. First one knee gave way, then the other. He went down in a lopsided kind of sprawl, and that was the moment I picked to hurl myself upon him.

He let out a yell, and drew a knife from his hip with a swiftness which said the play had been rehearsed and put into actual practice a thousand times, with a trip-hammer efficiency. But it couldn't have been too perfect a play, for the instant I planted a blow right under his chin his neck stretched out a foot and the knife went clattering.

To make sure he'd had enough, I knelt beside him, raised up his head, and asked him pointblank. He didn't answer me, and I saw that there was no recognition at all in his eyes. I decided that it would be safe to let him sag back, and go to sleep.

The instant I arose, the tallest of Ugly Face's two friends was right over me with a drawn gun. I'll say this for Number Two. Despite the massiveness of his shoulders, and his ill-proportioned wrestler's look he had a refined face.

Mild, almost baby blue eyes he had, and a mouth that was smiling almost gently at me as he took careful aim.

"I saw what you did to my friend," he said. "I can't let that happen to me, can I?"

He might have added, "It's a nice evening for dying, isn't it?" but I moved quickly to forestall him. I jackknifed upward, and caught him in the stomach with one sharply bent elbow, and the top of my skull.

He went down like a segmented plastic dummy, dropped from a cut wire in a garment display case. His knees folded, and he toppled forward and then back, as I lashed at his jaw with a sharp right, and delivered a left-handed blow to his solar plexus that almost broke my wrist.

He flattened out at my feet.

Number Three was still seated. I looked up quickly and saw that he was watching me, his expression strangely impassive. He was sturdily built, but far less formidable-looking than Ugly Face; I wasn't too worried about what might happen if he came at me with a knife.

I need not have worried at all. He either saw the gun lying at my feet and decided to play safe—or he just had no stomach for a stand-up, drag-out fight. But whatever he decided or thought, his behavior was incredible. He simply rose quietly from the table, nodded at me, and walked out of the tavern without a backward glance.

I swung about to face the two women. Agnes had leapt to her feet, and was staring at me with shining eyes. I looked at Claire, and was amazed to discover that her eyes were more puzzled than alarmed. There was no warmth in them; if she was relieved to see the two ruffians lying limp and unmoving on the floor, she gave no sign.

I felt suddenly closer to Agnes. She, at least, could share my alarm; I could reach her more quickly with an appeal based on simple common sense.

"We've got to find a safer place to stay," I said. "This was an ancient entertainment center. It still is—to men who think of women in only one frame of reference. You must have known that when you came here."

She nodded, her eyes searching my face. "Yes, I did. Does it disturb you so much?"

"Why do you ask me a question like that?" I flared. "If one of those brutes had started to paw you—"

A mocking look came into her eyes. "There was no danger of that. They had eyes only for Claire. I suppose I should feel insulted, but I happen to be a realist. If a man is primitive enough, a girl with Claire's kind of beauty will drag him down very quickly to the level of a savage with a bow and arrow, mounted on a wild stallion."

The mockery in her eyes grew more pronounced. "A woman must come to a place like this if she doesn't wish to be claimed too quickly. Few men would have the courage to come here alone, and for a woman there is safety in numbers, I knew you'd never find me if I hid myself away in an upstairs room, in one of the safer places."

"We've got to find a safe place," I said. "Immediately."

I turned to Claire. "When we leave here, we're going to walk very fast until we come to a place that looks safe," I said. "Do you understand?"

Agnes laughed. "You can tell, I suppose."

"It may sound crazy to you, but I can tell if a building *isn't* safe. Do you want to come with us?"

She looked at me steadily, the mockery gone from her eyes. "Just try and lose me."

Holding Claire's hand firmly, I walked to the door and kicked it open. It rasped on rusty hinges; for an instant, I feared that it might collapse. But then, slowly, it swung shut behind us.

I went out into the street again, with Agnes on my right, and Claire on my left, and no man ever had two more physically disturbing companions.

Of one thing I was convinced. Agnes couldn't know how I felt about Claire. Physically, Claire was the more perfect of the two; but there was that strange child-look in her eyes, the complete lack of adult understanding which chilled and disturbed me every time I glanced at her.

Agnes, at least, would have understood my desperation. She would have understood why I had turned to an android for warmth and sympathy—if I had chosen to tell her.

Did she suspect the truth already? I tried to read her expression for the answer as we moved along, hugging the dark, ancient buildings. But she hardly glanced at Claire, and her mind told me nothing. That, too, puzzled me. I had never before met a woman whose mind I could not penetrate at all.

Had she told me the truth about herself? Had she really come to the ruins in search of me? Was I that important to her?

In spite of Claire, in spite of myself, Agnes' intoxicating nearness overcame me for an instant, as it had in the vault, I had an impulse to stop, take her violently into my arms again, and tell her how glad I was that I had found her.

The building was gray and towering, with at least twenty vacantly staring windows and a great door. The feeling of security as we came abreast of it was strong in me, overpowering. I knew that it would be a safe sanctuary.

The power was so strong in me that I knew instantly that it was a building of numerous empty rooms. I knew that the rooms were huge, and littered with rubbish.

I had never been to the ruins before, but I knew that the building would remain safe for as long as our luck held. In the ruins, as elsewhere, men and women preferred a few, well-beaten trails. Nine-tenths of the buildings remained unoccupied simply because they were too bleak and forbidding to appeal to the human herd-instinct for proximity in danger.

I turned, and spoke to Agnes. "We'll never find a safer building than this We were lucky to have found it so soon."

I tightened my hold on Claire's hand, and we passed into a dark interior; we climbed a flight of narrow stairs to a double row of rooms, which ran along both sides of a dismal, refuse-littered corridor.

With the two women at my side I went into one of the rooms and shut the door.

It was huge and completely unfurnished, with cracked walls and a high, sagging ceiling festooned with cobwebs. Through the two dust-smudged windows we could see a patch of sunset sky.

There was an empty crate standing in one corner, still bearing a faded label: *California Figs.*

Claire sat down on it and looked at me. "Is this our new home?"

It was the most intelligent question she had ever asked.

I took her hand and pressed it gently. "Yes, Claire."

"She's taking too much for granted," Agnes said. "But we should be here long enough to get acquainted and reach a real understanding. There are a good many things I'd like to ask Claire."

She turned to me with the mocking look in her eyes again. "You won't mind, will you, if I share this room with Claire? You can sleep in one of the rooms across the corridor."

The request took me by complete surprise. It was a direct frontal attack, which I hadn't anticipated—more against Claire than against me.

I was tempted to put up a furious argument, then thought better of it.

Sleep across the corridor! In the ruins, that sort of thing was ridiculous on the face of it. If a woman couldn't trust a man that far, under circumstances so desperate, her presence in the ruins at all was a mockery and a sham.

But what could I say? How could I tell her that Claire needed looking after? Could I say: I don't want you to give Claire any ideas she can't assimilate without advice from me! I don't want you to confuse and frighten Claire with jealous woman talk. She's just a sweet, innocent child, and if you're going to start being callously inquisitive and prying you may inflict a grievous mental wound on her.

How could I tell Agnes that? If I encouraged her to start thinking of Claire as a rival, how could I know where it would end? How much would she find out about Claire if I left them alone together? Could she be trusted to look after Claire? The thought that the night might end in a violent quarrel, with Claire distraught and abandoned, was appalling to me.

But I decided that I'd be risking too much to make an issue of it then and there.

Could she be trusted not to harm Claire in any way? I decided to take the risk. I'd go across the corridor and leave the door of my room ajar. I was a light sleeper, and if anyone came into the building during the night I'd surely know, and wake up in time.

It was better than risking a jealousy flare up immediately. I needed sleep if only as a safety precaution, to keep my nerves alert.

I pressed Claire's hand again, looking defiantly at Agnes.

"I'll see you in the morning, Claire," I promised. "I'll be very near you. Do you understand? Agnes will see that no harm comes to you."

I whispered it, so that Agnes wouldn't hear. Then I turned back to Agnes. "There are a good many things I'd like to discuss with you," I said. "But they can wait until morning."

She smiled, and put both her hands on my shoulder. Before I could stop her she kissed me, so hard her teeth bruised my lips.

She stood back abruptly, triumphant mockery in her eyes. "Good night, John," she whispered.

Claire was staring at us both, her face strangely flushed. For the first time a curious, pained look had come into her eyes.

I went up to her again, and patted her shoulder.

"Don't be disturbed, Claire. That was just Agnes' way of saying 'Good night!'"

I turned then, and walked out of the room, Agnes' lips still burning mine. She had deliberately hurt Claire, derided her, and I hated myself for allowing it to pass.

The room across the corridor was as big, empty and dismal as the room I had left. It contained a broken-down chair, a small table, and a chest of drawers dark with mildew. The windows were shut tight; and the ventilation was so bad that it hardly seemed a fit habitation for the rats, which I could hear scurrying through the walls.

I tried to open one of the windows, and gave it up as a bad job. I was too tired to care. I lay down on the floor, and almost immediately fell into a deep sleep.

CHAPTER SEVEN

HOW LONG I slept I had no way of knowing. A vision of Venus Base was before me, I had my arm about the slim waist of a girl, and she was pressing close to me, and I could hear her excited breathing.

"Look down there, John," she whispered. "Kiss me first—then look."

A vision of Venus Base, and a woman's lips on mine, "Look down there, John. The men have courage, I'll grant you that; and the women are very beautiful. But they are traitors to society, and must be punished."

I saw her arm go out, white and slim. She was pointing downward, but I had eyes only for the whiteness of her flesh. I wanted to tell her how beautiful she was, and I was angry because she kept insisting that I concern myself with other matters.

"John, look down," she pleaded. "There are at least five thousand conspirators. Each must be identified and brought to justice. Tell me. Do you recognize any of the men below? Any of the women?"

I lowered my eyes at last to her bidding. Eight or ten couples were threading a narrow pass at the base of a cliff. The men wore Venus Base uniforms; the women were slender and very beautiful, with gleaming white shoulders and lustrous dark hair whipped by the wind.

They were heading for a rock cavern on the far side of the lake, and one man and a girl had run on ahead and were almost at the entrance.

Close to my ear a soft voice was whispering, "They are defying society, John, setting up a new society of their own where men will be free to choose their own mates in completely primitive fashion. Surely there is no greater crime against future generations!" The voice grew tender and cajoling, "We must fight them, John—you and I together. It was arranged that we should meet in the Computation Vault, and you have been watched ever since.

"Listen carefully, John. You were denied the right to marry so that you might become desperate enough to help Society fight this conspiracy. The raid on the illusion therapy shop was arranged so that you would bring Claire here and I could talk to you as I am doing now. There is a thought bond between us, John. It is a gentle thing and not compulsive. But you must hear me out, and I have come to you between sleeping and waking, and brought your mind close to mine so that there will be no barriers of mistrust between us."

I groaned and turned on my side, fighting the voice as a beguiling false thing that made no sense. But it did not pause. "You are under the hypnosis of love, John. Your need for me will make you forget Claire. When I kissed you just now I knew, I could tell. You will be permitted to marry, but I will be the woman you select. We will go to Venus Base together and fight this conspiracy. We will fight it with the aid of your extrasensory faculties. Society needs telepaths desperately."

I could feel her hands on my face, and the yielding pressure of her body against mine became startlingly real again.

Quite suddenly I was fully awake. The feeling of trance-like unreality and the agonizing helplessness was gone and I could see her face distinctly. I could remember kissing her in the twilight zone between sleeping and waking. I could recall every word she had said to me.

She had asked me to kiss her and my only thought had been to tell her how beautiful she was and to lift her up and carry her to a secret place and unfasten her dress and make violent love to her as her breasts slipped free.

But she had refused to let me do that. She had held out a promise of complete fulfillment, but first I must promise to do something which was unthinkable, which did violence to everything I believed in. She had asked me to help Society expose and destroy a conspiracy I knew very little about. I only knew I was in complete sympathy with the men and women I had seen in the pass. I would have gladly joined them and fought to the death to defend that kind of revolt, if what she had told me about it was true.

What did it mean? Had she attempted to implant in my mind a post-hypnotic suggestion, which I would be powerless to resist on awakening? Can a man be made to fight for what he hates, to defend a way of life that has become intolerable to him? Perhaps...if the rewards for an integrity-destroying betrayal are great enough. But I did not think I was that kind of man.

There was something else she did not know about me. To a telepath, a post-hypnotic suggestion has no meaning. Words whispered to him when he is in a trance-like state will be recalled when he awakens, with complete accuracy by his conscious mind.

That was just one of many things she did not know about me. But *what did I know about her?* Perhaps she had lied to me deliberately to test me, to find out just how deep-seated my rebellious impulses were. If I seemed to waver, to give even the slightest heed to a plea that should have made me turn upon her in rage she would know that I was not what I pretended to be.

In the vault she had shared my anger, had spoken out fearlessly, had not attempted to hide how she felt about a computation that denied her the right to marry. What if every word she had just whispered to me had been a lie and she was wholly in sympathy with the rebels in the pass? What if she were not just a fighter in the ranks, but a key figure in the revolt, an organizer? It was a possibility that could not be dismissed out of hand.

There was a startled look in her eyes, as if she had not expected me to wake up so soon. It vanished in an instant but the look that replaced it was just as much of a giveaway. I could see that she was disappointed. Frustrated and angry as well, although she did her best to hide it when she saw I was staring at her so intently I could hardly have failed to suspect what was passing through her mind.

She was wearing a sleeping garment, which she must have put on under her dress before coming to the ruins, for she had carried no garment bag with her. It was jet black, completely opaque, and even more abbreviated than the dress she'd taken off. It would have given her an almost death-harlequin look if her warmth and beauty had not completely dispelled such an illusion.

I wasn't sure what excuse she'd give for going to sleep in another room and waking up right beside me. I only knew that it would have to be a good one, for she would be forced to do a lot of explaining. Why had she abandoned a girl as young and fearful as Claire on her first night in the ruins, after promising me that she would look after her? And how could she explain away what she'd whispered to me in my sleep if I let her know, by word or look, that I remembered every word of that conversation?

I decided not to make it too difficult for her, to pretend that I remembered nothing and was just as surprised as she to find ourselves side by side on a floor thick with dust and cobwebs, with rats scurrying back and forth through the walls and the rafters overhead.

I pretended that I was still a little drowsy and covered up for the steady way I'd been staring at her by pretending to blink sleep from my eyelids and muttering an apology.

"I thought for a moment you were Claire. That sleeping garment—"

She cut me off abruptly, her voice tremulous with anger.

"She wears sleeping garments like this, does she? I was pretty sure you were lying to me about her. There's very little that girl doesn't know—about men and sleeping garments. I'm sure of that, I'm convinced she's considerably older than she looks—perhaps twenty-three or four."

"You've talked to her about it, I suppose? And just why did you leave her? You should never have done that. She's just a frightened child. Why did you come here, when you know how terrified she'll be if she wakes up and finds herself completely alone?"

"She isn't alone," she said. "She's with another man." She had gotten to her feet and was nodding toward the door.

I stared at her in stunned horror. For an instant it was too monstrous to grasp. It slipped away from me, went shrieking away into a nightmare world where cruel shapes with iron talons glared down at me out of a yawning gulf filled with nothing but darkness. She made no attempt to spare me.

"He was coming up the stairs, creeping up like a thief in the night when I went out into the hall to find out where the sound that had awakened me was coming from. I don't think he saw me, because there was only a faint glimmer of light and I flattened myself against the wall. He went right past me into the room, and shut the door. That was ten minutes ago. If she hadn't found him acceptable she'd have screamed by now.

"Oh, he could have clamped his hand over her mouth to keep her from crying out, I suppose," she went on quickly. "But no matter how brutal the men who come here are there is usually enough decency left in them to give a woman a chance to accept their lovemaking without resorting to violence. They seldom meet with resistance from the kind of women who come here, and vanity enters into it—"

In a nightmare when taloned shapes pluck and tear at your vitals the torment is often delayed, put off until you wake up screaming.

But I woke up quickly enough, I gripped her by the shoulders, swung her about and slapped her across the face, hard, I don't know why I didn't kill her. There is a rage you can't control, that backlashes in your brain like a whipcord— in so terrible, lacerating a way that the pain alone makes you want to kill.

"Why did you leave her?" I demanded, shaking her, coming close to slapping her again. "He couldn't have prevented both of you from screaming. You could have fought him off until I got to you."

She didn't seem to care about the slap. Her voice rose in sudden, desperate appeal. "John, listen to me. That girl is a freedom-ruin strumpet to her fingertips. It's written all over her. I know the type. Hard, calculating, not really needing a man the way most of the girls who come here do. It's an easy way of not working at all, if you're coarse-fibered enough. Women of that type even like brutality, seek it out. She gave herself away, because a woman like that knows that when she goes about with a wide-eyed, helpless look she'll appeal to the kind of man who is brutally sadistic, John, no woman could be *that* innocent. Surely you must realize it's nothing but a pretense to cover up what she really is."

I didn't let her go on. Whatever she may have thought about brutality, I gave her another sampling of it. It wasn't sadistic by *any* yardstick. It was just something she'd brought upon herself by what she'd let happen to Claire. I gripped her by the shoulders and sent her spinning back against the wall.

It threw her off-balance and forced her to sit down on the floor. The rage I'd felt was gone now. She no longer mattered to me, one way or the other. She'd jumped to a conclusion about Claire that was wholly cruel and unjustified, and had deserved the slap. But the only reason I'd sent her reeling back against the wall was to make it plain to her that I wouldn't tolerate her getting in my way when I crossed the hallway to the other room.

CHAPTER EIGHT

I KNEW it might be too late. What chance would Claire have of defending herself against a man who didn't even suspect that she was a child-woman who had never been made love to in an abrupt, brutally demanding way? How could she know what would happen to her if, in her innocence, she was more bewildered than angered and made him think that she would accept him as a lover if he abandoned all restraint?

The instant he turned brutal she'd have no chance at all. The shock would be too great.

He wouldn't be wholly to blame, if he thought she was the kind of woman Agnes had been talking about. But I had no intention of condoning him even that much. If he'd harmed her in any way he wasn't just going to end up dead. Unless he killed me first there'd be an ugly mess for the next tenant to clean up. A man with a bashed in skull—

I was just starting to cross the hall when the door opposite was flung open and he came out of the room with Claire in his arms. She was beating with her fists on his chest and her eyes were wild with fright. But he had clamped one hand over her mouth to keep her from crying out.

He didn't stop when he saw me, just increased the length of his stride and was a third of the way down the stairs before I could reach the top, the blind rage making me stagger. I moved just as fast as he had, but I had six feet of hallway to cross, and lost a second or two getting a firm grip on the stair rail.

I had to do that to size him up physically. When you hurl yourself at a giant with the sole purpose of crippling and killing him it's vital to know just how big he is and if there's a look of flabbiness about him.

If he looks flabby you hit him first in the stomach, putting all of your strength into the blow to jolt the breath out of him. Then you really set to work on him, pounding away at his kidneys and fielding right hooks to his jaw until he topples.

The trouble was…he didn't look flabby. He had the firmly knit build of a very large man who keeps himself in trim by exercise and doesn't allow any excess weight to widen his waistline and make him short-winded.

I'd caught only a brief glimpse of his face. But it didn't seem like a face that would change its expression and take on a scared look if the first few rounds of a fight went against him. He wasn't quite as ugly looking as the muscular six-footer who had come at me with a knife the night before, but only because his features weren't battered out of shape and defaced still further by a scar two inches in length. All in all, he was ugly looking enough.

But I didn't let his ugliness or the way he was built interfere with what I was going to do to him—unless he had a knife and managed to stop me by burying it up to the hilt in my chest before I could reach out and grab him.

He was out of the building before I reached the bottom of the stairs but I didn't let that deter me either. When a man is carrying a woman in his arms he can't move as rapidly as a man who is unencumbered and I caught up with him before he had gone thirty feet.

The light of dawn was harsh on his features as he turned to face me.

Claire was still beating with her fists on his chest, but he centered all of his attention on me the instant our eyes met. He stood very still, looking me up and down.

Claire was staring at me too, her eyes very wide. Suddenly she stopped struggling, and the terrified child look I'd expected to see in her eyes had either vanished or hadn't been that kind of look from the instant she'd started to struggle. Her expression seemed now wholly that of a grown woman aware of her peril, but overwhelmingly relieved and grateful that someone in whom she had complete trust had come to her rescue.

"You've made a bad mistake," I said. "She's my woman. If you put her down you'll have a better chance of making it my life or yours. Using her as a shield won't help you because there are holds I can clamp on you that will make you release her. If your arms aren't free you're going to be in trouble."

That wasn't strictly true, because as long as he held on to her I'd be at a disadvantage. I couldn't start working him over without running the risk of seriously injuring Claire. But I hoped he'd be too dumb to realize that or too enraged by the unexpected opposition he was encountering to think clearly. Just to have his claim to her disputed must have irked him, and in the ruins a struggle to the death to retain possession of a woman taken by force was so basic to survival that it made a resort to violence almost instinctive.

He wasn't dumb. But I'd guessed right about how he might feel about killing me or getting himself killed and settling the issue with the free use of his arms.

"She may have been your woman last night," he said. "But you might have a hard time proving that, because she's been fighting me like a wildcat. A woman who comes to the ruins knows what to expect and I've never before met one who would only let just one man make love to her. So I don't think she was your woman to begin with. There are women who won't let any man touch them. She seems to be that way, but it won't take me long to make a real woman out of her."

He narrowed his eyes and looked me up and down again. "I don't think you've got what it takes, chum. So she's better off with me. Why don't you just fade and give her a chance to become a real woman."

He was baiting me with the deadliest insult he could think of, and it convinced me that he had no intention of using Claire as a shield. He was going to set her down, all right, and do his best to batter me to a pulp the instant I closed in on him.

I was right on all counts, but my closing in was delayed for a second or two, because when he eased her to the pavement he took a slow step backwards, and kept a tight grip on her wrist.

"Get this straight," he said. "I'm going to let go of her, but she stays right here, where I can see her while I'm making you wish you'd taken my advice. If she tries to run I'll go after her and I'll have to hurt her—real bad. Is that clear?"

I knew that if Claire ignored the threat his rage might become so great that he would be capable of killing her. And I wasn't sure I could keep him from breaking away from me, even if I threw a hammerlock on him, and kept pounding away at his kidneys.

Much as it went against the grain I had no choice but to warn her. "Do as he says," I told her. "You're not to run. Do you understand?"

She nodded, the look of complete trust still in her eyes. "I will not run," she said.

"She catches on fast," Giant Size said. "I'll give you this much. She pays attention to what you say. It's too bad you haven't got what it takes to make her your woman. That's what I can't understand. Why are you willing to get yourself killed for a woman you can never hope to make *feel* like a woman. With me it's different. I've never met a woman yet I couldn't change, even the cold kind that pretend they hate the very sight of a man and clamp their teeth together when you try to kiss them."

"I'm going to change you in a lot of ways," I said. "Maybe you won't be so good at that when I'm through with you."

He let go of Claire's wrist and she moved back against the wall of the building next to the one we'd just left and a crazy thought flashed across my mind for an instant. Why hadn't Agnes followed us out and watched two men fighting over the kind of girl she'd been sure Claire was, even though it was the exact opposite of the truth. It should have given her a grim kind of satisfaction.

We started squaring off, and if someone had told me right at that moment that anything could have prevented what seemed certain to happen I would have accused him of believing in miracles.

It's always a mistake not to believe in miracles. I don't mean the wand-waving kind, but the way life has at times of playing fast and loose with the laws of probability.

When you've nothing but your bare fists to fight with you can surprise an opponent in two ways. You can lash out at him very fast, before he can come at you, or—you can hit him so hard he'll be too dazed to retaliate. I was getting ready to hit Giant Size so fast and hard he'd be staggered by the first blow when the miracle happened.

Around the corner, less than fifty feet from where we were standing, came two Security Police officers with compact little handguns jogging in black metal holsters at their hips.

I couldn't believe it for an instant, but in another way it didn't surprise me at all. I'd been half-expecting them to come into the ruins in pursuit of us, because when the sound of the sirens had died away in the abandoned subway entrance it had still seemed to be echoing in my ears and it had accompanied me along the blue-lit tracks and remained with me, at intervals, all through the night.

The moment they came into view I knew that they wouldn't want Giant Size to even try to kill me, because taking me alive would be of the utmost importance to them.

For a second or two I rebelled against the miracle and was almost sorry it had taken place, because I still wanted to do to Giant Size what he was hoping to do to me. But when more than your own life is at stake you've no right to resent an opportunity to split up the odds against you and turn the resulting confusion into a weapon that can give you the upper hand.

I didn't try to hide from Giant Size just how startled I was. I made a production of looking scared, and gesturing toward the corner in so alarmed a way that he'd realize instantly that the danger was too great to let a personal feud ruin our chances of staying alive.

Whether he had a knife or not I didn't know. I'd been prepared to have him come at me with a knife from the instant he'd set Claire down, but I was sure he knew that a knife couldn't help him now, for a Security Police handgun was a much more formidable weapon.

It was an intricate weapon as well, and it couldn't just be drawn and fired from the hip. You had to trigger and aim it and it took close to a half-minute to do that if you wanted to have a fair chance of bringing down a running target at a distance of seventy feet. And we could widen the distance by than much and more in twenty seconds if we ran fast enough.

"They haven't drawn yet!" I shouted at him. "They've just seen us. We've still got a chance if we can get to the end of the block before they open fire."

He either caught on as fast as I'd hoped he would or was way ahead of me, for he forgot all about what he'd threatened to do to Claire if she tried to escape the instant I swung about, gripped her by the wrist and we both broke into a run, heading for the cross street at the opposite end of the block. He broke into a run too, without even looking at us, his fear of the police making a fight to the death for a woman he coveted a luxury he could no longer afford.

I'd made one bad mistake, I'd misjudged by a few seconds the time it would take to reach the end of the block, and the first blast came when we were still directly in the line of fire and not around the corner out of sight.

I heard an agonized gasp close to me, and waited for Claire to sag against me with a constriction tightening about my heart. But she kept right on running, her hand so steady in my clasp I knew almost instantly that she was all right.

It was Giant Size who had been hit. He had fallen behind and when I looked back to see how bad it was he was down on his knees on the pavement, swaying slowly back and forth. He was clutching at his stomach, a look of bewilderment in his eyes. Blood was trickling from between his fingers and all at once the red glistening turned into a gush and he collapsed forward on his face. Apparently the bullet had gone right through him.

Another blast came then, so deafeningly close to us that it made my ears ring and I could feel the pavement vibrating under my feet. Then we were at the cross street and no longer in danger of being cut down by a straight-line blast. There was a piled-up mass of bricks and mortar extending outward from the building on the corner and the instant we were on the far side of it we slowed down long enough to catch our breath.

The third blast was followed by a clanging sound and a cloud of dust spiraled upward and hung suspended in the air above us for an instant. I tightened my grip on Claire's hand and we broke into a run again. The cross street was quite long, but we could see clear to the end of it. Our chances of getting to the end just by running were certainly not good.

There were a lot of branching side streets in the ruins and dark, weed-choked alleyways between buildings. Some were basement-level cul de sacs, or dead-end alleys terminating in brick walls too high to scale. But a few were open at both ends, and you could cross through them to a street running parallel to the one you happened to be on. If you were very lucky, you could even come out two or three blocks away, for there were passages that were like the inside of a horn. They circled around underground and doubled back on themselves, and you couldn't tell where you'd be when you emerged into the sunlight again.

We desperately needed to find that kind of passageway, because I doubted if coming out only one block away would save us. They'd see us turn into the alley and follow us…and you can be just as dead on one street as another.

They were shouting at us to stop now, warning us that they'd shoot to kill if we kept on running. But there were no more handgun blasts. I was pretty sure I knew why they were withholding their fire. They'd rounded the rubble and seen how long the street was and were confident of overtaking us. Either that, or they were putting their chips on the alleyways between the buildings, knowing that if we plunged into a dead-end one we'd be trapped with a vengeance.

Taking us alive would have pleased them better than killing us, I was certain of that, but the fact that they had blasted at all convinced me that if they had to kill us...they'd do it.

They'd killed the wrong man with a shot intended for me and had missed again before we'd turned the corner. But it could hardly happen a third time, for the Security Police were crack marksmen. It had been freakishly accidental, and must have infuriated them. In fact, their pride had taken so terrible a pounding they might well decide to forget the warning they'd just given us and blast anyway. Just knowing how easy that would be for them increased the feeling I had that our prospects of staying alive if we remained in the open were at a very low level.

I could hear their footsteps clattering on the pavement behind us, but I didn't look back to see how close they were. We passed an alleyway that ended in a high wall and another that was choked with rubble and bisected by an iron bar. But then we came to one that looked more promising, if only because it was completely uncluttered. I had no idea where it led. But it was the wrong time to speculate about the risks we might be taking if we plunged into it. They were shouting at us to stop again, their voices so loud now they could not have been more than a few yards behind us.

I tightened my grip on Claire's hand and whispered urgently, "Walk now...slowly. Stop running and walk. We must seem to be obeying them. Do you understand?"

"Yes," she said, her steps slowing.

"We're going into that alley," I told her. "Turn when I do—and don't let go of my hand."

We came to an almost complete halt before we turned. I wanted it to look like the first move in a surrender that would keep them from blasting again.

CHAPTER NINE

WE NEEDED only two or three seconds of grace and the strategy worked. They had no way of knowing we'd come to another alley and we were in the passageway and running again before we heard them cry out in rage.

The alley was open at both ends. Sunlight from the adjoining street glowed at the far end and we could see the glimmer before we were a third of the way through. We could also hear them shouting at us again, but they continued to withhold their fire.

The alley curved a little and was as dark as pitch and their reluctance to blast wasn't hard to understand. A few dislodged bricks from high overhead could have cracked their skulls, despite their protective headgear and in the ruins just a loud shout had been known to bring a ten-story building crashing down, its crumbling framework undermined by the vibrations alone.

We came out into a street as narrow as the one we had left. It was just about the same length and there was only one thing different about it that stood out. It wasn't deserted but was clamorous with sound, and the sound was coming from a careening fifty-passenger beetle filled with excited riders who were leaning out of the windows and shouting at the top of their lungs.

There was a frayed banner stretched across the front of the beetle but the lettering on it had a bright, recently gilded look. The lettering read: SIX-DAY BICYCLE RACE.

The beetle was coming straight toward us at so rapid a speed that I had less than two seconds to make up my mind. We could either leap aside and let it go careening past, or risk getting ourselves killed by grasping the guardrail and attempting to climb on board.

It was a risk either way, because if we leapt aside the Security Guards would be free to do exactly as they pleased about letting us go on living.

Coming to a quick decision was easier than making Claire understand, in just those ten seconds, what would happen if she failed to grasp the rail with both hands and hold on to it with all her strength while I leapt aboard ahead of her, bent over and lifted her into the vehicle by taking firm hold of her wrists. I couldn't have remained on the pavement and just hoisted her up. The beetle was moving too fast.

We made it. But if someone had asked me just how, when we were safely inside, breathing harshly and swaying back against the twenty-odd passengers who blocked the aisle, I couldn't have explained it to him. In a really desperate emergency there are reflexes which seem to take over while your brain issues automatic commands. If the beetle hadn't been moving quite so fast we probably couldn't have accomplished it, for even Claire seemed to realize how vital it was to make every second of exertion count.

All of the seats were occupied and the standing passengers filled every foot of aisle space. There were ten or twelve windows, but we could only see the occasional glint of sunlight on glass and were denied a view of the passing buildings as the bus continued on.

I held tight to Claire's waist as the bus swayed. It had all happened so suddenly it had left me a little dazed. The men and women around us were in an abnormal state too. But they were not dazed. They were shouting and gesturing and elbowing one another aside in an effort to see out of the windows. It made very little sense, because the bus was merely on its way to the races and it was too early in the morning for the streets to be lined with people.

It wasn't too surprising, however. They were almost frenziedly anticipating what they were about to witness, and

148

had to share their wild elation with every pedestrian who happened to be within shouting distance. A craving for excitement on the most primitive of all levels—that of a hunter stalking a jungle beast solely to bring it down and watch it die—had taken complete possession of them. What had once been a spectator sport had become something quite different, and if the bus had struck one of the pedestrians and killed him they would have rejoiced in the spectacle. They were powerless to stem the rampant brutality, which had been unleashed in them, and would have regarded the accident as a favorable omen, increasing the likelihood that they would not be disappointed when the races got under way and the death toll started to mount.

"Where are we going?" Claire whispered, her voice so low I could barely catch what she was saying. "What is a bicycle race? Are we still in—in danger? Does danger mean that we will die soon...unless the danger goes away?"

I thought for an instant she must have read the banner draped across the front of the bus. Then I remembered how often the words "bicycle race" had come to our ears just in the past three minutes, and realized how unlikely that was.

But could a child have grasped it so quickly, just by hearing the words? She must have associated a bicycle race with the destination of the bus very swiftly in her mind, for her question convinced me that she was both bewildered and frightened by her lack of knowledge of how dangerous a bicycle race might be.

I had no intention of telling her about the death toll. But before I could decide on the best way of keeping the truth from her without seeming to lie it came right out into the open at the far end of the bus.

There was a sudden commotion at the far end, and the pressure which was keeping us hemmed in became a violent jolting that hurled us back against the guardrail. It was as if someone far down the aisle had been hurled backwards and caused fifteen or twenty other passengers to lurch in almost as violent a way. You've seen it happen to a collapsing row of cards. You give one card a vigorous tap, and the entire row goes backwards as the tap is relayed from card to card.

The swaying and lurching of the passengers blocking the aisle was followed by a prolonged, agonized screaming. It went on and on until it was drowned out by an alarmed clamor and the shout of a woman who was clearly on the verge of hysteria.

"He's been stabbed! They were arguing about the races, and he whipped out a knife. The other one wrenched it from him and stabbed him twice. They were both standing right next to me."

"Where is he?" a man's voice shouted. "Why didn't somebody grab him?"

"He leapt off the bus!" the woman replied, her voice still raised in a shout.

"There's nothing much we can do for this one!" a third voice called out. "He's dead!"

"That could get us all in trouble!" The woman almost screamed the words. "The Security Police don't pay any attention to dead men in the streets. But a stabbing on a bicycle race bus is different. It has a socio-political look—"

"In the ruins? Don't be a fool, girl."

"I'm not a girl. I know what I'm talking about. I've seen the Security Police stop every bus at the track, to make sure the passengers aren't socio-political troublemakers, and didn't just come here to get themselves killed over a woman. I tell you, it could happen. It wouldn't be the first time, and not one of us would escape suspicion."

"The Security Police don't often come to the ruins," the man who had spoken first protested. "They're afraid to risk it. They know what could happen to them."

"Where are your eyes? We passed two of them a minute ago."

"She's right!" another passenger called out. "I saw them. We'd better toss him out right now, to be on the safe side."

"Are you sure he's dead?" someone else called out.

"We haven't time to make sure!" the woman shouted. "If there are more police at the track we may all be facing the death penalty, so why should we have any scruples about it, one way or the other? It makes no sense to me."

"We may as well make sure."

"Well…it won't take us long to make it official, if a few of you are that crazy. You there—and you. Take a look. See if his heart is still beating. Clear a space now. Let them get to him."

It all seemed like a mad nightmare. But in a nightmare you're often obscurely aware that you'll wake up before it is too late to find that the frightfulness could not have harmed you. But reality is never that merciful. Even when it takes on a nightmarish aspect you never get the feeling that you're going to wake up bathed in cold sweat, but with a wild gratefulness sweeping over you.

I wasn't sure I could hear the thud of the slain man's body hitting the pavement as the bus careened. But I could tell he was no longer on the bus by the abrupt silence which had followed the shouting a moment after they'd made sure that he was dead.

It was a callously brutal way of erasing all evidence of a crime. But it was a relief to know that the victim was beyond caring. If the man had not been dead and a few of the passengers had not been swayed by pity it would have been the kind of atrocity that can keep you awake nights, shaken and tormented by a depth of evil you don't like to think about.

I could almost hear the Big Brain mocking me, telling me what a fool I was. "Don't you know what human nature is like? Haven't you learned yet? When a man has ceased to follow my guidance there is no crime that he will not commit. Only my wisdom protects him, the scientific accuracy of every answer he receives to the questions he asks about himself. Without my wisdom to control him, waking and sleeping, he would become wholly a brute. If there were no tape recordings Society would become a jungle and every man would be forced to resort to violence solely to stay alive."

I had only one answer to that. It was not the kind of answer the monitors would have liked to hear, but I would have staked my life on its accuracy.

"A mechanical brain cannot think as a man does, or feel compassion for human suffering or understand the tragedy of unfulfilled desire. Thwart a man's basic impulses, deny him the right to love and be loved, and live his life to the full, and he will cease to stand upright in the sunlight and think of himself as man.

"But even when his spirit has been broken, his self respect shattered by a frustration beyond his capacity to endure, the flame of pity still remains unextinguished. It may dwindle to a spark and seem to disappear, but it never completely goes out. And that is Man's glory, and his triumph. Remember this. They did not hurl a cruelly wounded man from the bus to die alone in torment. They made sure that he was dead first. In only a few was compassion more than a spark. But the spark was in all of them, or the few could not have made their will prevail."

"How sure are you that the few will prevail if your own life is threatened," the Big Brain might have replied. "Turn and look behind you. Look into the eyes of a man who hates you for no sane reason. There is no spark of pity in him at all."

That, too, would have been a lie, for I had already started to turn and the Big Brain could not have known that I was completely aware of the man's malicious thoughts beating in upon me, and knew exactly why he hated me. When hate becomes that intense a telepath isn't likely to be deceived.

The man standing directly behind me hated me because he had seen Claire and knew that she was my woman, and her great beauty had filled him with envy and savage rage.

CHAPTER TEN

I TURNED SLOWLY, I wasn't sure he was one of the men who had tried their best to clear a space for us when we'd ascended into the bus, because the commotion had shuffled the passengers about a bit at our end of the guardrail.

The instant our eyes met I still wasn't sure, I only knew that I hadn't really taken him in before, because he had the kind of face you can't look at steadily for half a minute and ever completely forget.

His nose was blunt, almost snout-like, and his entire face had the kind of elongated look that you'll see occasionally in men whose simian ancestry seems open to dispute. *Piggish* was the word for it. But a pig, as a rule, is a docile, good-natured animal and the gimlet eyes that bored into mine were blazing with animosity.

It could have been just an accident of nature for I'd once known a gifted poet who had very much the same cast of countenance. But I was pretty sure there wasn't anything poetic about Gimlet Eyes. A poet can be filled with just as much animosity as the next man, if frustration rides him too hard. But imagination and sensitivity can usually keep animosity from boiling over. If I was any judge of character...sensitivity couldn't do for Gimlet Eyes what it could do for a poet, because I didn't think he had an apothecary's gram of it in him.

I wasn't so sure about imagination, because the first words he spoke seemed to indicate that he had covered all the angles.

"I saw those two Security Policemen too," he said. "They were just coming out of a between-building alley when you climbed on the bus. They couldn't have been more than fifty feet behind you. Maybe nobody else noticed how close they were to you. But I'm good at noticing things."

He continued to regard me steadily, a mocking smile on his lips. There was no need for me to probe deeply in a telepathic way to know what he was going to say next, because luck had dealt him a royal flush, or, at the very least, three aces.

He was about to turn the cards face up, so that everyone on the bus could see what kind of hand he was holding. But first he was going to threaten me, to prolong his moment of triumph a little and gloat over the way he hoped I'd look when he denounced me and started another commotion.

I didn't give him a chance to threaten me. "If you're smart you'll keep what you *think* you saw to yourself," I said. "They'll turn on you if they believe what I'll tell them—that you're a Security Guard. I'll say I saw you in the computer vault a few days ago. They won't stop to ask themselves whether it's true or not."

I paused an instant to let that sink in, then went on quickly: "There's something else I'll tell them. I'll say we were waiting for a bus to pass and when we saw that this one was overcrowded and wasn't going to slow down for us we decided to board it anyway. We didn't want to miss the first race, and were afraid the next bus would be just as crowded.

I'm sure they'll believe that—after I've tagged you with a Security Guard label. Think it over."

I didn't believe that there was much likelihood that he would, because the Security Police *had* been as close to us as he'd said, and a dozen or more passengers would leap to his defense the instant he jogged their memories. But it was important to find out how credulous he was, because what I had in mind if he refused to take the Security Guard threat seriously would call for steady nerves and the most difficult kind of bluffing.

He was the opposite of credulous. "What sort of a fool do you take me for?" he sneered. "If this bus wasn't on the way to the races you'd be lying in the street right now, as dead as you'll be five minutes after I tell them what I saw. Men on their way to the races don't use their heads much. They can see something that could get them killed—like two people leaping on a bus with Security Police right on their heels— and just go right on shouting their lungs out and thinking about what they'll see when they get to the track. But it will come back to them quickly enough, when once I've jolted some sense into them and told them why you climbed on board."

He was one hundred percent right, of course. The stabbing had made at least a few of them remember that the bus had gone careening past two Security Policemen emerging from an alley and it wouldn't take much to make them remember how close we'd been to the alley when we'd ascended into the bus at the risk of our lives.

There was still a chance that our ascent over the guardrail had passed almost unnoticed amidst the tumult and the shouting, for crowded buses were often boarded in that way. But the instant Gimlet Eyes started denouncing me there was no doubt in my mind as to what the outcome would be.

All I had to do was prevent him from denouncing me.

My small, experimental bluff had failed. But it was the big one I was counting on most and I told myself that it must not be allowed to fail.

I kept my voice low, because I didn't want the passengers who were standing close to him to hear me.

"Have you a knife?" I asked.

The question must have startled him, because his pupils dilated until Gimlet Eyes no longer seemed a very apt name for him.

"What makes you think I haven't?" he demanded.

"I was just curious," I said. "There's no percentage in carrying a knife if it isn't right in your hand when you're in danger."

I contracted my forefinger and jabbed the knuckle into his stomach just above his belly button, just firmly enough to make him think it was the blunt edge of a knife blade I was prodding him with.

"You're in danger now," I said. "If you shout or say one word that will carry I'll slash you up and down and straight across. Is that clear?"

Being forced to put it to him that brutally went against the grain, but I had no choice. It was no time for squeamishness.

He was standing so close to me there was no way he could have looked down to see the glint of a blade if it hadn't been just my knuckle I was prodding him with.

I could tell by his sudden pallor and the terror that flamed in his eyes that I didn't have to worry about his not believing me.

"All right," I said. "Now suppose you just ease yourself over toward the guardrail. I'll go with you. If you move as much as a half-inch away from me you'll end up dead. You're going to jump right off the bus when I tell you to make the leap. Do you understand?"

His lips moved but I couldn't catch what he said. It didn't matter, because he was so scared he nodded vigorously and the nod told me all I needed to know.

"Go about it in a calm way," I warned. "You've suddenly decided you don't want to go the track. You're fed up with the races. You've seen too many of them and you can no longer stand watching men die. But be careful not to look as if you were afraid of dying yourself. I'm not holding a knife pressed against your stomach. I'm just a close friend who is in sympathy with you but who feels that jumping off a speeding bus might be a little risky. He's doing his best to talk you out of it. Have you got that all straight in your mind?"

He nodded again, just as vigorously.

"All right, start moving toward the rail. One wrong move and you won't live long enough to do any talking.

We moved together toward the rail and I was careful not to let the pressure of my knuckle become less than firm. But that didn't prevent him from trying just once to save himself. He was clearly too frightened to risk getting himself stabbed by shouting or deliberately attempting to break away from me. But just as we reached the guardrail he drew his stomach in quickly, in a desperate effort to outwit me by widening the gap between his flesh and a knife that wasn't there.

If the gap had widened enough he would have probably swung about and grappled with me, counting on the suddenness of the move to swing the odds in his favor. But I thrust my knuckle so swiftly into the pit of his stomach that he grunted in alarm. He couldn't have looked more terrified if he'd felt the knife slicing into his flesh. Maybe he did, for the mind can play strange tricks on a wildly terrified man.

"Don't try that again!" I warned. "The bus will slow down a little before it turns the corner that's right up ahead. Jump when I tell you—and not before. I'm giving you every chance to stay alive."

I didn't think the other passengers would be too startled when he made the leap. Men on their way to the races behave in strange ways at times, jettisoning reason in a half-demented gamble with Death. Men had leapt off speeding buses before and sometimes for the very reason I'd impressed on Gimlet Eyes when I'd given him his cue. Quite suddenly the races lose their appeal. The death toll appalls them, and their only desire is to widen the gap between themselves and Death. Even the passengers on a bicycle race bus seem like accomplices of Death to them and they are seized with an uncontrollable impulse to escape, by hiding themselves in the anonymity of the ruins again. The instant they've leapt off the bus, they may experience a change of heart. But by then the bus will have passed out of sight.

The beetle was rapidly approaching the corner where I'd told Gimlet Eyes it would slow a little but I was far from sure that its speed would decrease. I was only sure that he'd be getting off, whether it slowed or not, because I couldn't risk giving him a chance to outwit me a second time.

Just before it reached the corner it swerved a little and that retarded it just enough.

"All right," I said. "Leap. You'll never get a better chance and I'm not giving you one."

He leapt straight out over the guardrail and I saw him land on his feet at the edge of the curb. He went reeling backwards, collided with a rusty spiral of metal that had once been a street lamp and was hurled still further backward by the graystone wall of the building on the corner.

I had no way of knowing whether he was seriously injured or not, because the last glimpse I had of him was too brief. He was just sagging to his knees when the beetle careened around the corner and I never set eyes on him again.

I didn't feel guilty about it, because it had been his life or ours. If he had denounced me, Claire wouldn't have been spared, I was sure of that. He'd been hoping to get me killed and claim her as his woman, but that only went to show dumb he was.

I elbowed my way back between the passengers at the rear of the beetle, found Claire and put my arm about her waist and held her firmly.

"We're safe now," I whispered. "Just trust me and don't become frightened. When we get to the track we'll disappear in the crowd."

"A bicycle race," she whispered. "What is a bicycle race like?"

I'd hesitated to tell her before the trouble with Gimlet Eyes had started, and I was still afraid to bring it right out into the open and try to explain it to her without window dressing.

What were the bicycle races like? You had to see one to really understand the depths to which human nature could descend and how terrible an unmasked, totally uninhibited glorification of barbarity could be.

What were the bicycle races like? What was the sadism of the ancient world you read about on punched metaltapes like... when the Big Brain was giving research historians the answer to questions they seldom asked? What was the ancient Roman Coliseum like?

Men and women by the thousands thrown to wild beasts. Gladiators, bloody-thewed, battling to the death solely to provide entertainment for an entire society turned decadent and accepting such brutality as a matter of course, without blinking an eyelash.

What was Attila the Hun's mountain of corpses like? And his wild horsemen of the plains? What would they have seemed like if you had been there and witnessed such horrors with your own eyes?

How could I tell her the full truth—or even a part of the truth?

A six-day bicycle race was supposed to be a sport, the sole surviving remnant of the great Age of Sports, which had reached its apex two centuries ago. But it was no longer a sport in a strict sense, because it had been transformed into a carnival of death.

It was another safety valve, permitted by the monitors and ignored by the Big Brain in a row of stippled dots when it was asked how Society could best protect itself from men and women who were driven by frustration to glorify death. The men who participated wanted to die, unconsciously at least, and the spectators could watch them die with the feeling that they were venting their hatred of life on sacrificial victims who were powerless to save themselves.

Technological brilliance is not confined to men in the good graces of Society. The most desperate and despised of outcasts may be a mechanical genius, and the bicycle races were the outgrowth of human inventiveness criminally applied. The changes that had been made in the bicycles alone—

I shuddered and shut my eyes for a moment and when I opened them again the stadium was just coming into view. But I saw Venus Base again before the careening beetle left the area of narrow streets and crumbling buildings through which it had been traveling and emerged on the wide stone highway which led directly to the track.

Several of the passengers had left their seats and crowded into the aisle, and we had been elbowed forward a little and could see directly out of one of the windows.

The tele-visual screen was a hundred feet square and it towered above the buildings on firm metal supports. It had been erected by the monitors in compliance with the Big Brain's instructions, three miles from the stadium and a short distance to the right of the open highway. It had been erected to serve as both an enticement and a warning.

It was almost as if the Big Brain itself had materialized directly in the path of the careening bus, and was advising the passengers to leave the ruins and accept a different kind of exile before it was too late.

"My wisdom can still protect you," the metaltapes seemed to be promising. "This is Venus Base. Men are freer here than they are on Earth. You will not be put to death if you return, and confess your guilt and ask to be sent to Venus Base. If there are too many outcasts—Society will be forced to move against the ruins and every man and woman who has rebelled against my wisdom will pay for their defiance with their lives. It may be later than you think."

But it wasn't the Big Brain we saw on the lighted screen. It was Venus Base in sound and color. I saw again the rugged plains, and the distant mountain ranges, veiled in purple mist. I saw the huge construction projects, and the clattering, earth-tunneling machines. I saw the breed of men I'd stood shoulder to shoulder with for two long years, lusty, brawling, authority-defying men, shouting their independence to the skies. I saw them leaving the construction site, with heavy packs on their backs, setting out across the plain for another construction camp. In a wilderness paradise perhaps, where they would be free to sit around campfires at night and break new ground in the first flush of dawn, free to lay the foundations of a new city with the certain knowledge that generations to come would be grateful to them and regard them as legendary giants.

No matter how great the tyranny may be under which he labors, you cannot take from a man that kind of glory, for no man lives in the present alone. The future is also a part of him, integrated into his bones. Even if he has no heirs who are flesh of his flesh, he adopts tomorrow's children and they become his heirs.

I saw the twenty rocket-launching pads, and the shining metal prefabs, barracks two hundred feet in length where a hundred men could lie on narrow cots and dream of a new tomorrow, when the newness and the bigness and the brightness would be increased tenfold.

I saw all that, and for an instant my heart leapt with joy. I had been a part of it, and could be a part of it again.

And yet— And yet—there was something wrong with it. There were men on the screen who could shout their independence to the skies. But nowhere were there any women. And how can a man take pride in his independence and proclaim that he is really free when he cannot make love to a woman, and feel her slender sweet body moving beneath him, and experience a rapture that blots out the present and the past, and makes only one moment seem eternal, as long as forever is.

CHAPTER ELEVEN

THE NEARER the bus swept to the lighted screen the more tremendous the tele-visual image sequence became. We saw the valleys between the mountains and snowy-plumed birds winging their way skyward. We saw the miles upon miles of jungle that dwarfed the rain forests of the Amazon, for every tree was as huge as a California redwood and was interlaced with blue and vermilion vines.

We saw emerald-green lakes and gleaming white beaches and two dozen jungle-encircled construction camps. We saw buildings in every stage of construction and fenced-in areas filled with rocket-transported supplies. We saw men bathing in the lakes, shouting and laughing and trying their best to convince one another that all was well.

But all was not well.

There were no women anywhere.

For a moment I felt closer to the passengers on the bus, for it was still their privilege to fight to the death over a woman and keep her for an hour or a day—if they were lucky enough to survive the flashing knife of an antagonist as desperate as they were for love, and just as reckless in his pursuit of it.

No women anywhere. No women at all.

Then I remembered Claire and how different it would be for me if I ever returned to Venus Base.

For me the image sequence on the lighted screen did have meaning, did hold out hope. Just how serious had my rebellion been? It had to be serious, or the Security Police would not have entered the ruins in pursuit of me. But could I still confess my guilt and return to Venus Base?

I had struck a Security Police officer in the performance of his duty. And the circumstances under which I had struck him had been unusual, adding to the gravity of the offense. An emotional illusion therapy shop was a dangerous place in which to strike anyone with the authority of the monitors behind him. And what if I had been under suspicion from the first and had been followed to the shop from the computation vault?

I had questioned my original computation and demanded another analysis and a third one after that, and I had just returned from Venus Base, where so much freedom was accorded a man that a marriage-privilege-denied computation should have seemed to him a small thing.

In the eyes of the monitors—this is a completely trivial limitation on his right to live his life to the full in the natural paradise that was being reproduced on the screen. That alone could have made me suspect.

But what if I returned and made a full confession, what if I accepted the promise the Big Brain seemed to be making to every man and woman in the ruins? What if my life was spared and I was permitted to return to Venus Base with—

With Claire? Would I be able to do that, even if I succeeded in concealing the truth from them? I would be watched twice as closely. I would be under constant surveillance. My very confession would keep them on the alert for any attempt I might make to take even a concealed weapon with me to Venus, let alone an android woman.

No, I'd have no chance at all. The promise was meaningless as far as I was concerned.

It was more than meaningless. To have gambled on it would have been a betrayal of everything I believed in. And suddenly, just as the bus careened past the enormous screen, I remembered what Agnes had said to me between sleeping and waking in the room where I had left her slumped back against the wall.

She had asked me to betray the men and women I had seen in the pass, had pleaded with me to turn traitor. And I had awakened to find her clinging to me, her lips warm against mine. But the instant she'd told me that Claire was in danger she had meant nothing to me and I had struck her in rage.

Was I less sure of what I had to do now, just because I'd seen Venus Base on a screen that was an ugly kind of propaganda attempt to make the ruin outcasts think that there was still a chance for them to exchange one kind of bondage for another? A worse kind of bondage, actually, because there were women in the ruins, and any kind of woman—even one who was a strumpet and a pawn to every man who fought to possess her—was better than no woman at all.

My thoughts returned to Claire again and just feeling the warmth of her slender body pressed close to me, and knowing how beautiful she was, strengthened my determination to remain a rebel, even if I couldn't be sure of outdistancing Death when I got close to the finish line.

The enormous screen was completely transparent, and even when the bus was on the far side of it I could see the images which were still making some of the passengers lean from the windows to get a better view.

And quite suddenly, the Big Brain did appear. The Venus Base scenes vanished and the many-tiered bulk of the Giant Computer filled the screen. I could see all of the winking lights and clicking computation circuits, and the triangular slots at its base into which the punched metaltapes fell.

It filled the screen for an instant and then receded a little and the entire computation vault came unto view. There were five tormented men and women in the vault, standing before the slots, but they did not look tormented on the screen. The monitors had made sure that they would look calm and assured, as if they had complete faith in the Big Brain's wisdom and would gladly accept what they read on the tapes, even if it condemned them to a lifetime of frustration and permanent exile on Venus Base.

Two Security Guards hovered in the background, with kindly expressions on their faces, their electro-saps well concealed.

I couldn't help wondering just whom the monitors were hoping to deceive. I was quite sure that every passenger on the bus—every man and woman in the ruins, in fact—had stood more than once in the computation vault and had seen how the Security Guards usually looked. I was equally sure they'd become ruin outcasts solely because they couldn't endure the way the future went blank for them when the metaltapes informed them there was no hope at all. Particularly when the guards nudged them with their electro-saps and told them that there were other men and women waiting to die inwardly and the space they were taking up no longer belonged to them.

When propaganda is nine-tenths a lie, the right words spoken with eloquence can sometimes make all of it seem reasonably sound. Someone down in the right hand corner of the screen was doing his best to make the passengers forget how they'd felt when a marriage-privilege-denied computation had come clicking out of the slot to fill them with bitterness and despair. But I couldn't hear what he was saying, because the bus had passed out of range of the screen's sound track. I could see the gestures he was making, and that was all. I wasn't even sure whether he was a monitor or a Security Guard. Possibly he was just a glib talker with no official standing who had been stationed there by the monitors to speak for the Big Brain.

At least fifty buses would pass the screen on the way to the races and some would slow down a little and catch more of the message, and a few would be traveling so fast the passengers would only get a two minute glimpse of Venus Base in full sound and color. But the monitors must have felt it would average up pretty well in its propaganda impact, for the enormous screen was the only new construction project in the ruins, and setting it up had been a risky undertaking. Fifteen construction workers, guarded by Security Police officers, had spent a week in the ruins erecting it. They had been forced to carry it in sections through an abandoned subway entrance, and along eight miles of track before it could be reassembled three miles from the stadium.

A half-ton of heavy equipment had been carried into the ruins as well, to make sure that the screen would be protected and that anyone touching it would be instantly electrocuted. So far no attempt had been made to demolish it.

The bus was less than a half-mile from the stadium now and I could see the crowds surging about the base of the big gray building. There were fifteen or twenty other buses in the parking area to the left of it, and four were just unloading. I could see the five projecting tiers, which completely encircled the building and the wide entrances with their clicking turnstiles on each level.

When I shut my eyes I could almost hear the clicking and it struck a chill to my heart, for it seemed like a clock with a red second hand ticking off the minutes that must pass before Death could take over and become master of ceremonies.

The passengers were all shouldering their way toward the rear of the bus in their eagerness to be the first to descend and it was hard for me to maintain my balance and keep Claire from being forced back against the guardrail. A man could protect himself with vigorous elbow jabs but a woman was in danger of being crushed if there was no one between her and the guardrail. I managed to keep her well away from it by gripping her arm tightly and rotating her slowly about as I interposed my shoulders as a buffer zone.

There was a wild shouting as the bus entered the parking area, and began to slow down, crossing diagonally from the gate to a cleared space about eighty feet from the stadium. It came to a jarring halt beside another bus that was no longer crowded with passengers. The driver was still at the wheel, however, and an outsized, corded-necked man was just getting off, carrying a struggling woman.

She was screaming and kicking but the instant he descended he slapped her face to quiet her and kissed her with such savage violence that she went limp in his arms. She made no further protest when he twined his fingers in her hair, tightened his hold on her and started walking toward the stadium without a backward glance.

A moment later I was also descending with a woman in my arms. Lifting Claire up and carrying her off the bus seemed the only way of making absolutely sure she wouldn't be injured in the crush. The passengers were in such haste to get to the stadium they no longer cared how violently they had to shoulder their way to the rear guardrail and leap to the ground.

A half-mile beyond the stadium, with its double spiral of tracks that extended for several hundred feet to the right and left of the massive structure, the ruins became an area of narrow streets and crumbling buildings again.

When I'd told Claire we'd try to lose ourselves in the crowd I had been visualizing that area as the one we'd head for, if we could get to it on foot without making ourselves too conspicuous. But the instant I set Claire down we were caught up in a surging crowd of passengers from two other buses, which had careened to a halt on opposite sides of the vehicle we'd just descended from.

It's easy enough to lose yourself in a crowd of two hundred shouting and shoving men and women. But it's the opposite of easy to keep from being swept along with it when it's moving in just one direction. We were right in the center of a crowd that had only one thought in mind, to get to the stadium as quickly as possible.

We were swept along and had no chance at all to move in the opposite direction or even fight our way to where the milling, closely packed throng thinned out a little. If I'd been alone I could have shouldered my way out, but with Claire to protect it was out of the question.

I made one brief attempt and gave it up as hopeless. We had to move with the crowd and trust to luck that before we got to the stadium we'd get a chance to clear a path for ourselves when the pressure behind us eased a little. A third of the shouting men and women would probably break ranks ahead of the others when we drew close to the turnstiles. Or so I told myself.

I was being too optimistic. More buses had drawn up in the parking area, some from the ruins on the far side of the stadium, and the crowd increased in density as we approached the turnstiles.

We were hemmed in with a vengeance. But that didn't mean we'd be forced to pass through a turnstile into the stadium. All of the spectators ahead of us would have to await their turn in single file, and before a turnstile could start clicking the rotating mechanism had to be firmly grasped and set in motion.

We could have rebelled and come to an abrupt halt before one of the turnstiles, forcing all of the spectators behind us to control their impatience. We could have insisted on our right to walk toward the stairway at the rear of the stadium, and ascend to the tier above, where there was another long row of clicking turnstiles with fewer spectators using them.

It would have caused a commotion and aroused a great deal of bitter resentment. But we could have gotten away with it. We could have ascended to the tier above and passed quickly along it until we came to another stairway and descended to ground level again. Then we could have mingled with a smaller crowd and left it unobtrusively and headed for the crumbling buildings a half-mile away with a very good chance of not being stopped by anyone.

We could have gotten away with it if I hadn't happened to glance upward and seen the four Security Police officers standing on the circular tier directly overhead, staring down at the crowd that was hemming us in. I'm not phrasing that in just the right way. The instant I saw the Security Police officers I knew we'd have had no chance at all of getting away with it.

For an instant I couldn't seem to breathe and my temples swelled to bursting. Then I remembered how close-packed the crowd was, and how hard it would be for them to get a good look at us from above when we were just two of several hundred people.

Even if we had to pass through the turnstile one at a time and become conspicuous for an instant there was a strong likelihood that they wouldn't recognize us. If we passed into the stadium quickly enough just the glimpse they'd get of us from that high above wouldn't be of much help to them. They'd just see the tops of our heads, for they'd be directly over us. Perhaps Claire's great beauty would give them an edge, because there's something about that kind of beauty that's hard to mistake, no matter how brief a glimpse you may get of it. But we had to chance it.

I put my arm around Claire's shoulder to steady and reassure her, without making any further attempt to resist the pressure that was keeping us moving forward so swiftly that the men and women in front of us were already advancing in single lines a few yards from the turnstiles.

"We're going into the stadium," I said. "Don't look up. We must pass through the turnstile as quickly as possible. Do you understand?"

"We will go into the stadium," she said.

"Yes," I whispered. "Through that turnstile right up ahead. I'll go first and the moment you come through I'll be facing you. Give me your hand instantly. We mustn't get separated, so don't let anyone come between us, and prevent you from following me. Watch what I do when I pass through. You press down on the long metal bar and the turnstile will begin to turn. It will keep turning until you're inside."

I stared into her eyes and was sure that she understood. There was no bewilderment in them or the slightest hint of incomprehension. But just to make doubly sure I added, "Turnstile-*gate*. We're going into the stadium through that gate right up ahead."

"Gate," she said. "We are going into the stadium to watch a bicycle race."

"We will have to watch them," I said, "to keep the danger from harming us. Are you sure you understand? Danger. You asked me what danger was and I told you."

"Yes," she said. "You told me."

I was afraid to let her pass through the turnstile ahead of me, because I didn't know how tumultuous the crowd might be inside. There was a greater risk of our becoming separated if she went first and was caught up in a swirl of people and swept along toward the track.

We didn't have to do much standing in line. For about ten seconds my heart stood still and I could feel the eyes of the Security Police trained upon me from high above. Then the turnstile started clicking and I was through, waiting to grab hold of her with a wild shouting at my back.

I died a little death just in the four seconds it took her to come through. She hadn't forgotten what I'd told her and I didn't have to grab hold of her. Her hand darted into mine, and we turned together to face a blaze of light and a clamor that was deafening.

CHAPTER TWELVE

WE STOOD at the base of the stadium's ascending tiers, staring down at the shining tracks and the swiftly pedaling cyclists. The tiers extended above us for two or three hundred feet and were almost filled to capacity. There were at least twenty thousand spectators in the two lower tiers and the upper ones were only a little less crowded.

I'd often wondered if the Big Brain, in the silent watches of the night, was not haunted by the horrors, which its metaltapes recorded. If a thinking machine can assemble and correlate the data in its memory banks, how can we be sure that it cannot experience emotion and be tormented by dreams it would prefer not to remember on awakening? And if the Big Brain had, in the midst of such a nightmare, coined a name for the races, might it not have been the one that came into my mind unbidden as I stared out across the track? ... *The Contest of the Deadly Cyclists.*

It was just barely conceivable. But I did not really think that the Big Brain could be nightmare-haunted. I was only sure that some of the monitors were, and knew on what dangerous ground they were treading when they buttressed their tyranny with that kind of safety valve.

The contestants rode furiously around oval tracks on vehicles very similar to the bicycles that boys and young men must have ridden through the ruins' narrow streets when trains roared through the underground tunnels and the subway entrances had provided a more rapid means of transportation to every part of a city that had not yet become a wasteland of crumbling stone.

I had seen three such vehicles in a museum of historical antiquities and the grotesquely shaped beetles which dated from about the same period and were even more popular as a means of transportation. Only the beetles looked odd, for the cycles still in use are much the same—two-wheeled, slender, pedal-propelled and gaudy with bright, contrasting colors and flying pennants.

The riders were armed with long, spike-like weapons and metal balls on a chain. If one of the spiked lances became enmeshed in the wheels of a racing cycle coming abreast of a competing rider, the man on the abruptly stalled vehicle would be sent hurtling through the air to land on the edge of the track, quite often with a fractured spine or fatal internal injuries.

To the spectators it was the penalty for defeat in a display of daring that merited thunderous applause and carried no stigma, since in every race some of the contestants had to lose and the vanquished, if they were lucky enough to survive, could become the victors in another contest.

The flying metal balls were even more deadly, for they were heavy enough when hurled with violence to crack a rider's skull and even decapitate him. But it was to the contestants' credit that they seldom used the metal balls with the intention of killing a competing rider outright before he could use his lance, but solely as a last-resort defensive measure.

There were accidents, however—failures in precision timing which could be ghastly.

What made the races so ancient-world barbaric was the spectator participation privilege. Soon after the race started half of the original riders were either so seriously injured that they were incapable of remaining in the race or were lying mortally injured at the edge of the track. At that point it was customary for a dozen or more spectators to descend from the tiers and leap upon the abandoned cycles.

The contest continued without further interruption until several more cycles were abandoned. The race went on for days. Each race was numbered and there were half-hour pauses between every third race to enable the victors to return to the tiers and be embraced and accepted as mates by women who had come to the ruins expecting to be fought over. That a bicycle race victory was more to an outcast woman's liking than a knife-wielding victory by a man who could not hope to win such acclaim was hardly to be wondered at, for it flattered their vanity and gave them a wider choice of mates.

The race that was just starting had already caused two bicycles to go spinning from the track and a third to overturn. One rider was lying sprawled out at the edge of the track, his limbs grotesquely bent and another was stumbling toward the tiers with a look of agony on his face. His right arm dangled and just before he reached the tiers he swayed and had to be helped up the steps a little to the right of where we were standing.

No one need envy a telepath. I was not only almost tormentingly aware of how the cyclists felt, but the emotions, which the spectators were experiencing, beat in upon me in tumultuous waves. Deep in my mind a thousand voices seemed to be clamoring to make themselves heard.

I could usually close my mind to thoughts I did not wish to share, by making a deliberate effort of will. In fact, telepathic communication was largely like a two way street. The traffic moving in opposite directions seldom collides if the street is wide enough and if you're driving in a beetle you have no opportunity to communicate with the passengers in the swiftly passing cars.

You have to be moving in the same direction as the mind you wish to tap and unless the wish is present the thoughts of others seldom sweep through your mind like a tidal wave.

But it happens sometimes, when you're in the midst of a very large crowd swayed by emotions that are tumultuous and completely uninhibited.

I could barely endure the thoughts of cruel anticipation and the murderous rage that goes with frustration and a craving for the release from tension which the witnessing of a barbarous spectacle seems to bring about in some people.

Not in me. But the tidal wave was so all-engulfing that for a moment the way I normally thought and felt went spiraling away from me, into dark depths that were shark-infested. A wave of revulsion surged up in me as I fought against that tide of malignancy and hate. But I knew also how the most brutal of prison guards felt when they were free to inflict irreparable injuries on the helpless men and women in their charge.

High up in the tiers a woman was thinking, "If he is killed watching him die will give me pleasure. But if he kills the opposing rider that pleasure will not be denied me, for the defeated man will be the one I will watch die. Then he will return to the tiers in triumph, with grievous wounds that he will make light of, and take me into his arms. I will not resist him, for his triumph will be mine. Death and love. What more could a woman desire?"

And in another part of the stadium a man was thinking, "In a moment I will descend to the tracks. It will be *kill or be killed* and I do not care too much which way the scythe swings when Death decides that a big sleep is the best cure for one of us. Do I really want to go on living? A woman? That's a cure too, and I came to the ruins looking for one. But maybe Death is better. In half the books you find in the ruins, in libraries choked with dust and rubble, Death is a woman. Why shouldn't Death be a woman? To die is like going back into a big, dark womb, isn't it? That's what Death is all right—a woman. I've known it all my life."

And still another man was thinking, "I'll swing the metal ball straight at his head before he has a chance to mesh the wheels of my cycle. I'll brain him. Sure, they'll be a protest. If I do that and return to the tiers they may kill me. Well—let them try. I'll go down fighting, laughing at them. I'll laugh until my lungs burst. Bad sportsmanship is what they call splintering a rider's skull before he has a chance to do it to you. What a joke that is, when you think about it. They don't know the meaning of sportsmanship. I've seen it once or twice on a metaltape when the Big Brain is punching out big words as a cover-up for what it has done to us. Goes back to the big Age of Sports. Baseball, football, boxing. But in those games you didn't get killed so often. You could afford to give good sportsmanship a twirl."

Then, quite suddenly the cruel, oppressive thoughts were gone, and other thoughts impinged on my mind. A far-off voice seemed to be whispering to me, urging me to leave the shark-infested depths and swim with vigorous strokes sunward. Sunward through the brightening water until the last lingering trace of darkness vanished.

"We are very close, you and I, because I am your biogenetic norm woman," Claire seemed to be whispering. "I know you even better than you know yourself. You would never welcome Death and turn away from the sun. You love life too much.

"Beauty you love and the great sea when it breaks and the wonder of a woman in your arms, her eyes misting with ecstasy as you caress her. You would never surrender your birthright."

I turned and stared at Claire in stunned disbelief, and for a moment I found it impossible to accept that kind of miracle. How could I accept it when her eyes were still those of a bewildered and frightened child and she was clinging to my arm as if I were her only support in a world that was the opposite of childlike.

But surely no one else in the tiers could have sent such thoughts winging toward me. They were not the thoughts of an outcast woman who had suddenly decided I was just the right man for her. How could such a woman have known what I looked like even—one distant man in a multitude? Even if she had been sitting in the lowest tier and could see me clearly, would she have spoken of herself as my biogenetic norm woman?

There was one way of making sure. I could turn stern and hold Claire at arm's length and ask her why she had lied to me from the first and pretended to be a child-woman. And if she refused to say a word or went right on lying I could read the truth in her eyes.

Or could I? How could I be sure that she wasn't more skilled in the art of deception than any woman I had ever known?

Still—I had to know and it was the most promising way of getting at the truth that I could think of. But before I could look at her accusingly and try to make her realize what a tragic barrier deception could erect between a man and a woman, a wild burst of shouting swept over the tiers.

Two more riders had been hurled from their cycles and the lance of one was still spinning through the air. But it was not that double defeat which had caused the spectators to leap to their feet in wild excitement. It was the collision of a third rider with one of the stadium's high stone walls. His cycle had gone completely out of control and the impact of the collision had hurled him back against the wall with such violence that a dark stain was spreading across the stone as he slumped to the track.

Scattered across the track were three discarded lances and two metal balls, one of them still attached by its chain to the outflung wrist of a badly injured rider. He was writhing in pain and trying to get up, and another rider had stopped pedaling for an instant to avoid crashing into him.

There was a tele-visual screen projecting outward over the upper tiers and so strategically placed that all of the spectators could see it. It was not a Big Brain propaganda screen, but had been erected by the strong-willed men whose constructive genius had rebuilt a crumbling stadium and kept the races an unchanging freedom ruin sport for two full generations.

There are always men who must exercise authority and keep the rules from being broken, even in a freedom ruin. It does not matter if the rules are barbaric, the activity over which they exercise control the most brutal of sports. They must seize power and hold it—or perish.

It was as if the Big Brain had whispered to them: "You are outcasts and exiles. But you can still make men obey you if you can maintain absolute control over a freedom ruin sport that has become as indispensable as the most pernicious of habit-forming drugs to every man and woman in the ruins.

"The races are a safety valve which must be preserved. And because for men like you a marriage privilege and the right to make love would be meaningless if you could not also exercise power and make yourself feared, you have no choice. You must help me to preserve this safety valve. You are not just a ruffian sulking in a dark alleyway, but a stadium builder. You walk about with guards at your side and are protected from violence night and day. And some outcast women are very beautiful. There are rewards, which only a stadium builder can claim. You have no choice, because you are what you are."

There were many such men in the ruins. They had kept the tracks in repair, the bicycle race beetles running. But I did not admire them.

CHAPTER THIRTEEN

THE SCREEN had been blank when we'd entered the stadium. But now, quite suddenly, it lighted up, and the head and shoulders of a black-uniformed man appeared in the midst of the radiance, his thin, sharp-featured face creased by a frown.

He waited for the shouting to subside a little, then raised his hand to enforce a silence, which would enable him to make himself heard.

His voice was harsh and deep-throated and the magnification of sound provided by the sound track caused it to reverberate throughout the stadium like a steadily beaten drum.

"These are the rules," he announced. "They must be obeyed by all of you, riders and spectators alike. Every spectator is privileged to participate, but remember—there are only fifty cycles. If you are a spectator you must await your turn. You must also be one of the few lucky ones.

"You must wait until twelve cycles have been overturned before you descend from the tiers and claim your spectator privilege. If a dispute arises in the tiers and more than twelve of you attempt to descend to the tracks you must settle it among yourselves. But remember this. Only twelve spectators will be permitted to descend to the tracks at anyone time.

"At the base of every stairway the supervisors have stationed men armed with handguns who will blast you down without compunction if you disobey the rules. Only twelve spectators will be permitted to cross the tracks when a race is in progress, even if more than twelve riders have been unseated."

He had failed to mention that that particular rule was not always rigidly enforced, because a cycle lying riderless at the edge of the track grated on the spectators and made them resent the fact that fewer riders would die. Sometimes as many as twenty spectators were allowed to cross the tracks and leap upon the abandoned cycles. But no rule in any sport is ever rigidly enforced when it goes against emotions that basic. I had put my arm around Claire's waist and knew that she was trembling.

I seemed to hear again the clicking metaltapes as the Big Brain answered the most puzzling of all questions—why a rule becomes strengthened when expediency makes it just a little elastic, "A rule must never be permitted to impose a tyranny that is absolute. Rules are made to be broken—up to a point. It must be made to seem that generosity is being exercised, a broad and understanding tolerance, a winking and a secret elbow-nudging as the rule is stretched a little.

"Men and women must be made to feel that the monitors are very human too and would not be above stretching a rule or two themselves if they thought they could keep it a secret. The monitors—or the men who enforce rules in a freedom ruin. Completely human and generous-minded, with a deep understanding of human needs and aspirations.

"Even the need to be brutally inhuman when watching a brutal spectacle in a freedom ruin when decadence has taken over must seem to be sympathized with and understood by the upholders of the rules. 'There's a little sadism in all of us, chum. Don't think we're any different from you in that respect. So go ahead and stretch the rules a little. We'll look the other way and don't think we won't be secretly envying you. We're all in this together. It's your sport and our sport and the only reason we have rules is to keep a sport like this from disintegrating. You want to keep it brutal, don't you? Well…so do we. But we know more about such things than you do. If you don't have rules the brutality will become chaotic and the entire sport will fall apart.'"

As I said once before, the Big Brain wouldn't have phrased in precisely that way, because the Big Brain's wisdom is always Society-orientated. The Big Brain would never have quoted ruin outcasts, even if they happened also to be stadium builders. Unless, of course, the Big Brain itself had a hidden rebellious streak and could fall asleep and have nightmares. I've mentioned that before too, as a possibility it would have been hard for me to take seriously.

The man on the screen had paused an instant, as if he'd said enough about the danger the spectators would be running if they stretched the rules too far, and was about to give them some less threatening instructions.

When he spoke again his voice had lost its harshness, "Remember—the races will continue for six days. Five, or six thousand of you will have an opportunity to participate. Not all of you came here to participate and there is no stigma attached to remaining a spectator."

A half-smile appeared for an instant on his lips, as if he wanted the spectators to think him a man who could unbend in an appealingly human way, and did not hold humor in contempt.

"I am quite sure," he went on, "that many of you have found women greatly to your liking. You would have nothing to gain by exchanging a woman you've risked your life to possess and who is properly grateful to you, for a woman you know nothing about. If you will permit me to be blunt— most men who participate in the races do so with only one thought in mind. They will return to the tiers with the certain knowledge that their strength and daring will have given them a victor's privilege and they will enter a contest that will end in another victory...that of the bridal couch. Or am I mistaken about that? Every man must answer for himself, for what man can be sure of victory when he is alone with a woman in the dark? Perhaps that is the most dangerous and uncertain of all contests. I have won many such victories in my life, but if I were to tell you of the defeats—"

The man on the screen seemed carried away for an instant by an impulse to turn the screen into a confessional and bare all of his wounds to the public gaze, by disclosing every closely guarded secret that had tormented him across the years. He quite obviously had what the ancient Freudians would have called a Casanova complex. For when a man is willing to confess that he has often met with defeat in his lovemaking, he is hoping to convince everyone that his victories have been so numerous that he can afford to be completely honest in that respect.

For an instant I felt a twinge of pity for him, for there is a little of that egotistical absurdity in all of us.

He saved himself by what was clearly an effort of will that he found difficult to maintain, for he had to lower his eyes for an instant to pretend to himself that there were no spectators watching him and a confession would have been wasted on long rows of empty stone seats. A shudder passed over him and the half-smile vanished from his lips.

When he spoke again he was once more in command with himself and talked as a rule-upholder should, in a precise, matter-of-fact tone.

"When you enter the contest you'll have enough freedom of movement if you just strip off your outer garments. Some riders may prefer to strip to the skin and the rules permit it. But it is the opposite of wise. An inner garment protects you when a glancing blow might otherwise lacerate the skin over a wide area. It's just as well to take every reasonable precaution."

I wondered why he cared until I remembered what I'd said on the bus in reply to the Big Brain when I'd seemed to hear the humming computers mocking me. Something had prevented the passengers from hurling a fatally wounded man from the bus to die alone and in torment on the pavement. They had insisted on making sure that he was dead first.

The man on the screen was not wholly without pity. It had dwindled to a single glowing ember, perhaps, but it was still there.

"Don't keep too close to the edge of the track," he went on in the same matter-of-fact voice. "If two riders come abreast of you at the same time, raise your voice in protest, and wave toward the tiers. They will be forced to abandon their cycles and will be subject to the death penalty.

"Remember that your prime objective is to mesh the wheels of your opponent's cycle with your lance. He has the right to try to unseat you by striking you on the body—but not on the head—with the flat of his lance, below the spiked tip. He must not deliberately aim the lance at your head, throat, chest or any part that could fatally injure you. And when your own wheels are meshed you must observe the same rules of combat.

"But if you should be unseated, if your cycle is overturning, you may deal blows of a more dangerous nature. That is your right as a last-resort defensive measure. You may even hurl the metal ball. But even in so desperate an extremity you must not aim at his head or try to kill him. The justification for such a rule of combat may seem strange to you. But it is not without a basis in logic.

"The risk of receiving a mortal injury at your opponent's hands must be present. That risk alone makes the contest what it is. Without the constant risk, the certain knowledge that you may be killed at any time by a blow aimed too high or too low—not deliberately, but with miscalculation—there would be no glory in victory. A contest such as this must test a man's courage and steadiness of nerve to the utmost or it becomes a hollow mockery."

"But what if they're not killed, just seriously injured," a voice said, so close to me that I thought for a moment it was Claire who had spoken. Then I realized that no woman could have had a voice so deep and resonant, even if she had been a virago. It was a man's voice, with nothing womanly about it.

Before I could turn and look at the speaker he went on quickly: "What fools they are. What incredibly blind fools. A crippling injury is a high price to pay for a moment of punch-drunk recklessness. If you have to drag yourself back to the tiers with a fractured spine you'll no longer be thinking what a privilege it is to have your pick of a dozen or more women. There are injuries that can make a man wish that he *had* been killed. He said nothing about what happens when a cycle's wheels are meshed and the rider is hurled to the track, or back against the walls of the stadium."

I turned then and looked at him. He was big, with the boyish look about him that often goes with a bear-like massiveness in a man even when he's over forty. He had deep-set blue eyes and tousled light hair that straggled down over the right side of his face as if he'd been facing into a windstorm and hadn't had time to brush it back with his hand.

He brushed it back abruptly, and I saw that he had a very high brow.

"You're new to the ruins, aren't you?" he asked. "Is this the first race you've let them sell you on?"

I stared at him, hoping he wouldn't suspect how much the question had startled and alarmed me. What had made him so sure I was new to the ruins?

"What makes you think I haven't been here a month—or two or three years, for that matter?" I demanded.

He grinned then, just as abruptly as he'd brushed back his hair and I saw that he was looking at Claire.

"All that time—with a woman like that? And no one killed you and made off with her?"

"How do you know I didn't take her away from another man an hour ago?" I countered, my temper rising. "Two can play at that game. You can fight for and claim and lose a woman again four times a week. And you don't always end up dead."

I hated myself for being forced to answer him in that way, because I didn't want to think of Claire as a woman I'd just fought for and could lose again, even if it wasn't true. I had fought for her against the man who had tried to take her from me, even if it hadn't been with a knife. But it went against the grain just to lie about any part of it, because I couldn't endure picturing myself taking Claire away from a man who had been her lover before me. Fitting her into that kind of mind picture was hateful to me. In a way, it was an insult to Claire.

But I was just angry enough to want to hurl the statement he'd made back into his teeth, to prove to him how wrong he could be, and how stupid it was to jump to a conclusion about me with so little to base it on. And it was important to find out, too, if he was lying and really did have something more solid to base the conclusion on.

There was no way I could find out, for he dropped the argument I'd started as if it had suddenly ceased to interest him, and apologized in the friendliest imaginable way.

"You're right," he said. "I like to think I'm pretty good at character analysis. Most people have some one thing that's a little special or different about them, and you can usually tell a great deal about them just by observing them closely. But not always. It's a kind of game with me. But it's quite unlike the game that is being played down there."

"There are no other games like that one," I said. "In the ruins or on Venus Base—or anywhere."

He looked at me steadily for a moment. "Have you been to Venus Base?" he asked.

I saw no particular reason for keeping it a secret. If he was good at character analysis he probably knew anyway, for you can't disguise the way Venus Base construction workers pronounce certain words. There's a slight accent change, and the words have a distinctly different ring to them, as if the wind and the sun and the rain had made the speaker want to sing or waltz about and shout at the top of his lungs. It's a change you adopt unconsciously when you've been on Venus Base for as long as two years.

"I wish I were there now," I said. "If you've never been to Venus Base you don't know the meaning of freedom. There is no real freedom in the ruins. A man is not free when Death is pacing him at twenty feet or breathing down his neck, and he must kill to stay alive."

I'd picked a strange time to speak my mind that openly to a total stranger, when men were dying right before our eyes, and the tier that arched above us was a swaying sea of spectators with sharks weaving in and out in the shallows. But somehow he no longer seemed a total stranger. I had suddenly found myself liking him.

It was a strange time to bare my inmost thoughts to anyone. But if I'd picked a different time I wouldn't have been thinking of Death with quite such an intensity of loathing and staring straight down at the tracks, and I would have failed to see them before it was too late. Not just two or three Security Police officers, but thirty!

They were advancing along the high stone wall at the base of the stadium a few yards from where the tracks ended, and two of them were already climbing the stairs, which ascended to the lower tier.

The pair on the stairs saw me before I could turn and move further back into the crowd. I was sure of it from the way they stiffened and their hands darted to the gleaming metal holsters at their hips.

My first thought was of Claire and whether she'd realize how fast we'd have to move to lose ourselves in the crowd before they got to us. Just the fact that they'd recognized me so quickly convinced me we'd have to move very fast, because they would feel outrageously cheated if they were unable to clinch that advantage, like hunting dogs within sight of a quarry they'd spent hours in tracking down.

I'd forgotten all about the big man at my side I'd suddenly found myself liking. But he hadn't forgotten me.

His hand shot out and fastened on my wrist. "We'd better drop the playacting," he said. "I know who you are and why the Security Police are after you. I'm telling you that because you're going to have to trust me."

He must have known what two such jolts in the space of half a minute could do to a man who had to think fast and clearly, because he went right on talking with a blockbuster kind of urgency. "They'll blast you apart if you don't get moving. Head for the stairs on your left, and descend to the track. There are ten discarded cycles down there now, and that's close enough to the number you're supposed to see lying overturned before you start down."

His fingers bit into my wrist. "If you just cross the tracks and leap on a cycle as if you had every right to enter the race they'll be afraid of angering the spectators by blasting you down. If you wait for the rush to start you won't have a chance. But if you head the rush your boldness in taking such a risk will encourage the others to follow your lead. I'm absolutely sure they'd never open fire on that many participants, when there are ten cycles lying overturned. But you'll have to be the first to put it to the test."

He was blueprinting it for me, all right—even if he didn't fully realize just what a setback the Security Police would get if I mounted a discarded cycle and stayed on it until the end of the third race. I was sure for a moment my thoughts had gone racing on ahead of him by that much at least. But it was just a mistaken idea I had.

"If you can unseat ten or twelve riders and stay in the race you'll be lifted up when you get back to the tiers and carried on the shoulders of the spectators all the way to the top of the stadium. It happens about fifteen times in every race, and if the Security Police tried to break in on that kind of celebration and take you out of the stadium under guard they'd be massacred to a man. They're risking their lives just by coming here."

If I'd been alone on the tier what he was urging me to do would have made sense. But with Claire to consider there was a fatal flaw in it. The Security Police wanted both of us, and entering the race without knowing whether she'd managed to disappear in the crowd would have been just another way of dying.

He had a solution for that too. "She'll be safe enough, I promise you. I told you I know who you are. It shouldn't take a telepath long to find out just how much trust he can place in a promise."

I turned and looked steadily into his eyes. There was a moment of torturing uncertainty when I felt I couldn't be sure, and then—I was sure. Completely, with every doubt swept away.

The promise he'd given me he'd keep—unless the odds against him became overwhelming and he could save neither Claire nor himself. For some reason I could not fathom he felt honor-bound to help me, even at the risk of his life. But I still might have hesitated if he hadn't said, "You spent last night in the ruins. On the second floor of a four-story building. There was another woman with you. Her name is Agnes. She had a tiny transmitting instrument concealed in her clothing. The message wasn't intended for us, but we intercepted it. Can you find your way back to that building?"

There were a dozen Security Police officers on the stairs now and the first two had reached the tier and were elbowing their way toward us, slowed down a little by the shouting spectators at the top of the stairs.

"I can find it," I said, knowing I'd just have to keep in mind how closely it had resembled a funeral vault when I'd left it.

"All right, that's where you'll find us," he said. "Now get going!"

I drew Claire close and whispered, "We'll be together again soon. I want you to trust this man and do exactly as he says. Do you understand? *You must trust him.*"

"I will...trust this man," she said.

I turned then and headed for the stairs on my left, not daring to look back, fearing that just the thought of parting with her would become unendurable and I'd jeopardize the only chance we had of staying alive and going to Venus Base together.

He'd guessed right about everything. I had to resort to some close to brutal elbowing to get to the stairs on my left and five enraged spectators awaiting their turn in line made a grab for me. But I fought my way past them and was halfway down the stairs before the Security Officers on the other stairway saw me.

I had a bad moment as one of them leveled his handgun and then seemed to change his mind about blasting. He would have been asking for trouble if he'd opened fire on me across sixty feet of intervening space, and blasted down three or four spectators. Just getting me would have put him in about as much jeopardy, because of the way it would have looked from the tiers.

A moment later I was at the foot of the stairway and

the armed upholder of the rules standing there could have shot me down without running the slightest risk of killing a spectator, I was within ten feet of him. But there was a shouting right behind me. His eyes were on the stairs and he must have realized that the rush had started. He was so torn by indecision that he couldn't move at all.

Then I was past him and heading straight out across the tracks toward the nearest discarded cycle, stripping off my outer garments as I ran.

CHAPTER FOURTEEN

THE CYCLE was lying at the edge of the track fifteen or twenty yards from the high stone wall of the stadium. The Security Police officers might still have been thinking of throwing caution to the winds and blasting me down before I could start pedaling. But it was a possibility I refused to let unnerve me.

I covered the distance fast, running in a steady, natural way without straining to increase my speed.

I reached the cycle before I came to the only discarded metal ball that was not chained to a dismounted rider's wrist. I grasped the cycle by its handlebars and raised it from the track, and the instant it was vertical I ran on with it, letting the wheels spin without attempting to mount. When I came to the metal ball I swooped, attached the dangling chain to my wrist and headed for the nearest discarded lance.

I was fully armed when I mounted and rested my feet on the pedals, casting a swift glance behind me. A spectator who had been the first to follow me out across the tracks was now in undisputed possession of another cycle which had been lying a little beyond the one I had headed for. But it had taken him longer to arm himself and mount, and the cycle he was on was now the nearest one to the tiers and about forty feet behind me.

The spectator-turned-contestant was lean and muscular, with unusually long legs and a rugged, craggy-featured face. He appeared to be about thirty years of age.

I did not like the way his muscles rippled and the firm set of his jaw. There was no particular reason for the sudden mistrust I experienced when my eyes swept over him—only a vague premonition that I was looking at a formidable adversary who would come after me fast and give—and expect—no quarter.

I did not wait for him to start pedaling. I swung out into the middle of the track and entered the race as a fully armed and forewarned contestant, keeping firmly in mind the rules, which the man on the screen had stressed.

The cycle was easy to manage—a remarkable vehicle that seemed almost to propel itself. The slightest touch on the steering apparatus was sufficient to keep it on a circular course around the track, which was several hundred feet in circumference.

The chain on my left wrist in no way interfered with my riding and permitted me to move my steering arm freely. It was an extremely light chain, but undoubtedly it possessed sufficient tensile strength to make the metal ball the deadliest kind of weapon. The ball itself, which was far heavier, rested by my side on the seat. In my other hand I held the spiked lance, half-poised and in instant readiness.

I tried not to worry too much, to put out of my mind the thought of a pursuit and engagement, which was certain to be quickly forthcoming. I resisted an impulse to look back and concentrated on the pedaling, casting only the briefest of glances at the riders immediately ahead of me.

I knew that with luck I might outdistance Long Legs until he himself was overtaken by another rider and his vehicle overturned before he could come abreast of me. I had seen that happen. In fact, one of the contestants had been in the race from the beginning and had been a steady, continuous victor whom no one could unseat.

That solitary, victorious rider had been overtaken eight or ten times, but each time he had put on a superb performance, meshing the wheels of the pursuing vehicles with an agile twisting of his lance. Twice he had hurled the metal ball just as his own cycle was overturning and managed to bring the vehicle swiftly back into equilibrium again.

Speed—speed was really the secret. It was also the most difficult problem the riders had to contend with. The cycles speeded up and slowed down constantly and it was hard to control the speed with accuracy, because each of the cycles responded instantly to the slightest acceleration in the pedaling.

There was always the danger that your speed would become too great, and you'd lose control of the cycle, leave the track and go crashing into a stadium wall. You had to slow down abruptly at times in self-protection, and that gave the rider directly behind you a better chance of overtaking you. All he had to do was stay alert and increase his own speed just as you slowed.

No matter how skillfully he pedaled every rider was certain to be overtaken sooner or later—once, twice or a half-dozen times.

I had forgotten for a moment that the main purpose of such a contest was to test a man's courage to the utmost and that he was supposed to think only in terms of striking skill and aggressive action.

My most important adversary, the one I must try to unseat as quickly as possible, wasn't the one who was coming after me with a similar deadly purpose in mind. If I was overtaken Long Legs would, of course, become my most immediate and important adversary. But until that happened it was the cyclist directly in front of me I should be concentrating on.

The contest was not primarily a flight from danger with each cyclist thinking of himself as a possible victim, with the need to keep his wits about him in a desperate struggle just to stay alive. That psychology could be fatal. It was a "fox-pursued-by-hounds" psychology and could sap a man's stamina and capacity to survive before he got started.

It took skill to outwit a pursuer and a fair measure of courage as well, but that courage and skill must not be contaminated by fear. And the best way to keep fear at bay was to go on the offensive and work up a steady, controlled rage against the cyclist immediately in front of you.

Maybe that rage should not even be controlled. Maybe it should take complete possession of you, become savagely destructive and as primitive as the jungle night.

But could you work up that kind of rage against someone whom you had no reason to hate? I didn't know, because I had never tried it.

Could I make myself believe that the cyclist directly in front of me had done me a great and irreparable wrong—a wrong that would not be avenged unless I killed him? Not just unseat him and send his cycle spinning but deal him a mortal injury.

Wasn't it just barely possible that a rage so great would give me a feeling of strength and supremacy that would enable me to laugh scornfully and deal him a lesser blow—a blow that would bring him down but not prove fatal?

Would that work? Could that kind of rage ever be less than wholly destructive? When reason was completely absent could a man so enraged ever be capable of sparing his victim?

Well...and why not? Grit your teeth and begin to hate. You dislike the cyclist ahead just on principle. You don't like the set of his shoulders, the color of his hair. Give reason a slight rein at first. Justify your dislike to yourself.

Then forget about reason. Don't you see? Your hate is getting stronger. You don't need reason any more. Forget about it entirely. You've got it cooked. Your rage is becoming a splendid, barbaric thing. You don't need to have any reason for hate. What ever made you think you needed a reason, what ever gave you such an idea in the first place? Hell, everyone has to fight to stay alive, doesn't he?

I shuddered and set my lips tight. I just couldn't do it—couldn't work up that kind of rage against anyone, let alone the cyclist in front of me!

But I knew I'd have to work up some kind of rage if I hoped to survive at all, *because the cyclist directly ahead of me was—Winner-Take-All.*

I couldn't just shut my eyes and pretend he wasn't there, the contestant who had been overtaken eight or ten times and had sent as many cycles spinning with an adroit twist of his lance.

Thirty feet of gleaming track still separated us, for he hadn't slowed down once. For a full minute the distance between us neither lengthened nor shortened and that must have annoyed him, for quite suddenly he turned his head and stared back at me.

I could see the harsh set of his features as the sunlight slanted down over him, but what angered me the most was the look of cold animosity in his eyes. He had never set eyes on me before, but he'd made a very good job of convincing himself that he ought to hate me. If it had been a savagely primitive kind of rage it would have angered me less than the cold, calculating way he'd allowed pure venom to spill over in his mind.

I stepped more firmly on the pedals and my cycle shot forward with a speed that startled me. The distance between us diminished to twenty feet—and then to fifteen. The whir of the wheels was loud in my ears, louder than the beating of my heart. I fought against an impulse to clutch the steering apparatus tightly, realizing just in time that a too firm grip would have started the cycle zigzagging and perhaps sent it hurtling from the track.

Winner-Take-All straightened in his seat, clearly aware that I was about to overtake him. He could have increased his own speed by stepping on the pedals as hard as I had done, and lengthened the distance between us to twice what it had been. But he chose not to do so.

His neck cords were stiffening now and his lance arm was in swift, preparatory motion. But an instant before I swept abreast of him he glanced back once more and that was a mistake. He had to turn swiftly again to steady his cycle, and I picked precisely that moment to strike.

I could see the glint of terror in his dark eyes as my lance meshed the back wheel of his cycle and brought it to a grinding halt.

He had only one chance to save himself, and he did not hesitate to resort to it in the life-endangering way that was sternly forbidden by the rules. As the cycle teetered and hung poised he raised himself a little and hurled the metal ball, aiming it straight at my head.

The black lash of the chain made a shining arc in the air and if I hadn't ducked the instant I'd seen the ball coming it would almost certainly have splintered my skull.

The rage I'd fought against and didn't want to feel was boiling up in me now. Maybe there are times when a man has no choice, when he has to let the caged savage loose.

I didn't wait for his cycle to overturn. I descended to the track and hurled myself upon him, gripping him by the wrist and dragging him to the track, chain and all. I used the chain as a weapon, raising his wrist and lowering it as I brought it forcibly into contact with his skull. I was careful not to let him slug himself too hard—just hard enough to prevent him from getting to his feet and hurling the ball at me again.

I stopped the instant he slumped and I was sure that he had blacked out.

Between us we'd made a big rent in the rules and I had no idea how the spectators were going to feel about it. I could only hope the supervisors at trackside had noticed how close he'd come to killing me when he'd hurled the metal ball. If they had and were convinced it wasn't an accident all they'd have to do to clear me and keep the spectators from becoming enraged was activate an electronic circuit and the man on the screen would announce that Winner-Take-All was a loser all the way. When he woke up he'd be facing a death sentence and all I'd get would be a disciplinary reprimand for descending from a cycle voluntarily, which was also a violation of the rules.

I didn't really think they wouldn't see it as an accident—if they'd noticed it at all. But I was wrong. They activated the electronic circuit and the man on the screen started to talk about it with anger in his voice.

He didn't get far, because the applause had already started and it became thunderous before he'd spoken twenty words.

I'd never heard anything quite like it. It was a wild ovation that shook the tiers, and made the tracks vibrate. It was so tremendous that it stopped the race. The riders drew in to the side of the track and dismounted and the armed men at the base of the tiers had difficulty in keeping several hundred spectators from descending to the two stairways and swarming out over the tracks, headed in my direction. A few of them actually got past the upholders-of-the-rules and were running toward me.

It stunned me for a moment, until the machinery of my brain started moving again and I began to understand what had set it off.

Winner-Take-All had covered himself with glory. To unseat ten or twelve riders in just one race was a feat that probably had never been equaled before, let alone surpassed. And when a man has been built up that way his admirers don't like to think that they've been completely taken in and that he is a coward at heart. When he'd hurled the metal ball straight at my head they'd seen him for what he was.

Disillusion and rage had made them transfer their allegiance to me. I'd dragged a popular hero down from his pedestal and slugged him unconscious with the chain at his wrist. And I'd meshed his gears before he could score another victory in a contest of skill.

I wasn't particularly proud of what I'd done. For a moment I had let the caged savage loose. It had been his life or mine and I'd acted solely in self-defense. But still the savage had helped me, and I was sorry I'd been forced to let him out of his cage. He exists, I suppose, in every man but I still wasn't proud of what I'd done. The quicker he was hurled back into the cage again the better, and if I could starve him to death on a bread-and-water diet for the rest of my life so much the better. But the spectators had no way of knowing how I felt.

I was popular hero number one now, and for an instant I was still too shaken to fully realize what it meant.

Then I grasped it in its entirety and knew exactly what it meant. The crowd would lift me to their shoulders just as the big man had predicted before I'd descended to the tracks, and carry me to the top of the stadium and there would be a stairway leading straight down from there to the entrance gate and I could be through it and on my way to rejoin Claire without running the slightest risk of being stopped by the

Security Police. I'd be a popular hero all the way down and my only problem would be to keep so many admirers from accompanying me down that it might slow up my progress a little.

And that's the way it worked out. Only—I didn't even have to square my shoulders and walk calmly back to the tiers, like a popular hero everyone was proud of—except myself. The spectators who had managed to get past the guards were suddenly taking firm hold of me and lifting me up and I was carried back with the thunderous applause still echoing in my ears.

The applause went on and on, but a half hour later I could no longer hear it, for I was out of the stadium and threading my way through a maze of narrow streets toward the building where I had spent the night.

CHAPTER FIFTEEN

THE STREET did not seem quite the same when I came to it and stared down its rubble-strewn length, and the building where I'd spend the night looked more bleak and desolate—perhaps because the sunlight was beginning to wane a little and the crumbling piles of masonry on both sides of it had a reddish, almost sanguinary look.

But I was sure it was the right street, the right building. You can't easily forget a building and a street where you've had a close brush with Death, and a woman you'd have trusted with your life has been guilty of treachery and betrayal.

Two women—and one had gone out of my life almost as quickly as she'd entered it and the other had stayed with me and not gone out of my life at all. But I'd lost them both in different ways, because when a woman is no longer at your side and you don't know what has become of her, you've lost her.

Would I find them both here, Claire and the man who had promised to protect her? If he hadn't been overconfident and the promise had been kept the nightmare would be over for an hour or a day, with no guarantee we'd be spared another one. But if he'd failed, if the Security Police had blasted him down, the nightmare would never lift, for Claire would be lost to me forever and I would never know what had become of her.

The street was deserted, but I paused for an instant before entering the building to make absolutely sure that I hadn't been followed. A few feet to the right of me a gigantic rat scurried into a crevice in the masonry and bluebottle flies were making a buzzing sound where the pavement sloped to a patch of exposed soil.

A dead starling lay on its back in the middle of the unpaved patch, its plumage still iridescently gleaming and the flies were just settling down over it.

On Venus Base there were no starlings, dead or alive—or rats either, for that matter. It was of no great importance but when a man is under tremendous tension, thoughts that are ordinarily trivial and meaningless seem to take on an obscure, half-mysterious significance.

Perhaps it is the pulse of nature, of all life everywhere that we become aware of at such moments, making us realize how close is the link between living and dying, and how little basic difference there is between a man with the blood warm in his veins and a dead starling.

I ascended the stairs slowly, because there is a time for haste and a time when it is better not to hurry. There are disappointments so bitter that few men can endure them without crying out in torment, and it is well to steel yourself in advance when such a disappointment may be awaiting you.

So I climbed the stairs slowly, step by step, and the nearer I drew to the floor above the less sure I became that I would ever see Claire again.

She opened her eyes then and looked at me. Her arms went around my shoulders and her breathing quickened and there was no need for words between us to make us aware that we were alone in a miraculously intimate way. Not only was the world shut out, it had ceased to exist. *We* were the world, as all lovers are when a blazing intensity of emotion enables them to create a new universe of light and fire.

She shivered a little, tilting her head back and opening her lips as I loosened the gold clasp at her shoulder and parted the outer garment which she had worn on awakening in the Emotional Illusion Therapy shop and never taken off.

I removed it now, with fingers that trembled a little and let it fall to the floor.

"Darling," I whispered. "My life and my bride..."

I need not have feared that there was a metal band under the garment and that her body was not as I had hoped it would be.

She was all woman.

Later, as she was putting the garment back on again, her eyes were shining as she reclothed the beautiful body that had been made for me alone.

She spoke then, for the first time. "He told me that you would not be killed. He could not wait here with me, because there are others who must be protected, and barely time to make sure that we will not be in danger again. But he told me that you would come back and I would be safe here if I locked the door and waited for you without making a sound."

She smiled then. She had never before smiled, in all the dreams of my youth and I had never fully realized just how beautiful a biogenetic norm woman could look when the universe became all light and fire, and every barrier to complete fulfillment had turned into a gateway to the stars.

"I would have locked the door but the key would not turn. I would have kept on trying to turn it, but I was so afraid that you would never return that what happened to me seemed not to matter very much."

She paused, as if searching in her mind for just the right words to make clear something she feared would seem incomprehensible. I knew exactly why people will sometimes feel that safeguarding themselves can be postponed, but I let her go on.

"You asked me to trust him and I did. But how could he be sure that you would not be killed? And if you did not return I would have died too. And I stopped trying to turn the key because I had begun to die a little and when you are dying you do not always try very hard to stay alive. You do not really want to die. But you are not sure than life is any better than letting yourself die, because when you are dead there is no longer any torment. I did not intend to stop trying. But I was in such torment that I had to lie down and close my eyes and let myself die a little more. I thought if I did that I might find the strength to turn the key. So much of me would have died that the torment would not have been so great—"

I nodded. "I know how it feels to die that way," I said. "You don't have to explain. There isn't a very wide gulf between sleep and death and you needed the help of both. I felt the same kind of torment coming up the stairs, not knowing whether I'd find you here or not. Maybe that's why I found the strength to turn the key."

"The door was still open, so you must have turned it after you came into the room," she said. "I am glad that you did that. You were locking out the world because you wanted to be completely alone with me. That's why you turned the key."

"I was locking out the kind of world you find in the ruins," I said. "I was locking out the Big Brain, and the monitors. Well, yes—I was locking out all of the other worlds as well."

"Even Venus Base?" she asked.

"Even Venus Base," I said.

I suddenly remembered that I hadn't said one word to her about my two years on Venus Base. And there was so much that she would have to know, because if we lived to see another sunrise I'd be taking her there.

The knocking wasn't very loud and for a moment I wasn't sure that another flurry of wind hadn't swirled up the stairs and caused the door to creak a little on its rusty hinges, for sometimes just a creaking can sound like a succession of swiftly repeated knocks.

But I wasn't left long in doubt. The knocking became louder and more insistent and a voice called out with sharp impatience. "You may as well let me in. The Security Police will be here in a moment, so you have nothing to gain by keeping the door locked. If you're wise, you'll listen to what I have to say. Or would you prefer to wait until the police get here and break the lock?"

If it had been a voice I had failed to recognize I would not have opened the door. But it was a voice I had heard in the vault amidst the hum of the Big Brain's computation units and the night before whispering to me between sleeping and waking. It was the voice of a woman I had struck in anger, because she had violated a trust by using another woman as a pawn and had been guilty of a double betrayal.

Anger rose up in me again and I walked to the door and turned the rusty key that had locked out the world for me. I opened the door wide and Agnes walked into the room.

She stood very still for a moment, staring from me to Claire. She held herself in a tense, arrogant way, as if she welcomed this chance to release her pent-up feelings and had the authority now to threaten us with more than words.

"I was sure that you would both return to this building," she said. "When you left here this morning you escaped from two Security Police officers by boarding a bicycle race passenger beetle. You escaped again at the stadium. The man you met at the stadium helped you. He brought Claire to this room and told her to lock the door and admit no one.

"Oh, it was all very cleverly planned. The man who helped you is a criminal conspirator, a rebel. He intercepted a message I sent to the Security Police last night, but because he is not a telepath—as you and I are, John—he did not know that you had left this building until he intercepted a Security Police alert which informed him that you were at the stadium."

She was looking directly at me now. "He's had specialized training in undercover spying, and had no difficulty in finding you, even in so huge a crowd. He knows exactly how to scan a crowd with electronic magnifying devices, and a woman like Claire stands out.

"He helped both of you to escape, by bringing Claire here and urging you to enter the races before the Security Police could place you under arrest. I was probing your mind when you descended to the tracks and it was all very clear to me. I had left the ruins and was in the computation vault, making sure that every step we are taking to crush the rebellion will be in strict accordance with the Giant Computer's instructions. But if I had been at the stadium I could not have been more sharply aware of everything that was taking place there, because I was probing his mind too.

"You're a remarkable man, John. He must have been as sure of that as I am—or he would never have urged you to enter the race. He must have thought you'd have a very good chance of winning the kind of victory you'd need to make the spectators turn on the Security Police in rage. He couldn't have known, of course, just how remarkable that victory would be."

I shook my head, because I wasn't flattered by her praise. Somehow it angered me.

"It was blind luck," I said. "The rider whose cycle I overturned made the mistake of looking back to see how close I was just as I came abreast of him."

"It takes great skill and steadiness of nerve to take instant advantage of a mistake like that," she said. "You have exceptional qualities of body and mind and you're making a tragic mistake in wasting them on a woman like this, and joining a conspiracy that's certain to fail."

I had an answer for that one too. "If you're so sure," I said, "how do you square a rebellion that's certain to fail with a man who was more than a match for the Security Police? There must be other men just as extraordinary on Venus Base, or the conspiracy would have been smashed before—"

She cut me off abruptly. "Then you do admit that you're an extraordinary man?"

"Not at all," I said. "I'm talking about the man who helped us and who doesn't seem to be here now."

"You know as well as I do that a telepath can't always trace a man's movements with complete accuracy when he's doing hardly any thinking at all, just concentrating on getting to his destination as quickly as possible. I knew he'd be bringing Claire here, but the visualization contact broke down right after he left the stadium. He's familiar with the ruins and didn't have to stop and look around him, and visualize this particular part of the ruins to get here, I didn't think he'd get here quite so fast or leave quite so quickly. It was a natural enough mistake under the circumstances. Just the fact that he escaped in time—and even what he accomplished at the stadium—doesn't make him extraordinary."

Her face had lost its harshness and she seemed, quite suddenly, almost to be pleading with me not to go on accusing her. "John, I will say it again. It is you who are extraordinary. I knew it from the first—when we stood side by side in the vault and you took me into your arms. You talked wildly, rebelliously—even scornfully. You derided the Giant Computer, denying that it cannot make a decision which is not wholly wise and in the best interests of Society.

"John, listen to me. You talked rebelliously, but I knew that deep in your mind you did not really feel that way."

"If you knew that," I flung at her, "why did you lie to me? Why did you pretend to agree with everything I said and make me think—"

"Make you think what, John?"

"That your anger was greater than mine. When I talked about Venus Base in a less harsh way, you were more derisive than I had hoped you would be. For I was less honest with myself than I am now, and did not quite want to believe that women would never be sent out..."

She moved closer to me and a look of almost desperate appeal came into her eyes. "John, suppose I told you I had a reason for lying. Suppose I told you that Society is so dangerously threatened that it must ignore what an extraordinary man says and continue to believe in his capacity for loyalty. If the rebelliousness has not gone too deep, it may not be too late. He may still be able to save himself."

CHAPTER SIXTEEN

I LOOKED at Claire and saw that she was standing motionless, staring at Agnes with her lips tightly compressed.

If she was startled by what the other woman had just said, she gave no outward indication of it.

I would have gone to her and put my arms about her if I had not been so sure that what Agnes had said would not make Claire less sure of my loyalty to the world we had shared together.

Agnes must have sensed that too, and suddenly she realized that words alone were not a woman's only weapon, for she swayed toward me as if she were about to fall and almost instinctively I reached out to steady her. It was just about the most foolish thing I could have done, for it gave her a chance to cling to me and wrap her arms about my shoulder—so tightly I could not have unclasped them without an effort that would have seemed brutal even to Claire, angered as she must have been.

"John," came in an insistent whisper. "John, listen to me. *Do you really think that Claire is an android?*"

There was a sudden stillness between us, as if the words themselves had a fateful quality and she dared not go on too quickly.

Her embrace became a little less clinging, but I was too startled to grip her by the wrists and force her arms to her side.

"Oh, it is all so clever, John, so carefully planned. The conspirators select reckless young spacemen, cut off from life and fulfillment by what they shrewdly but falsely call the tyranny of the Giant Computer. They appeal to them through the android shop scheme. Don't you see, John? The rebel women pretend to be androids.

"They *pretend* to be androids, John. The biogenetic norm data of each pilot is carefully examined in advance and women who conform to the data of individual pilots are sold to that man in the shop. The women have to keep up a skillful pretense of having child minds.

"Until they are in space, John, and the pretense can be thrown aside. Then the pilot is told. Since the woman conforms in all respects to what he has always sought in a woman he is not likely to turn back. If he is human, he is not likely to regret having thrown in his lot with her. If a woman is beautiful enough there is no folly a man will not commit for her sake."

For an instant the dream experience of the night before seemed almost to be recurring, for I felt myself, for the barest instant, to be remote from the room in which I was standing and even from the woman who was whispering to me.

But this time I was inside a cave—vast, shadowy and filled with smoke. Human figures moved waveringly through the gloom, I saw a man with his head bandaged, a woman supporting him. There were crimson stains on the bandage and his hair was a solid mass of clotted blood.

Some of the men were seated; others stood straight and resolute in shafts of reddening sunlight. But each was accompanied by a woman, and each had the look of a seasoned fighter struggling against desperate odds to preserve his independence and self-respect.

"Society is keeping the struggle secret, John. It has just begun, but it is spreading fast. So far, we have contained the rebels, have driven them from the central camps to solitary outposts. But reinforcements keep pouring in. The android shop scheme is working dangerously well.

"A hundred spacemen arrive daily, and the women inspire them in the struggle, stand by their sides through bloodshed and despair. Eventually, we will have a formidable army to repel."

I awoke completely then from the strange spell. The cave vanished, and was replaced by the firm contours of reality.

At first I saw only the dim oval of Agnes' face, a white and moving blur. Then she moved her head a little more, and the three inches which had separated her eyes from mine, widened to five or six, and I could see all of her features distinctly.

"You must listen to me, John," she pleaded. "You must believe me. I, too, have unusual extra-sensory faculties, as I told you. When I shut my eyes, scenes not clear to the senses present themselves to me with a startling clearness. I can see scenes on Venus Base now, just as you have seen them. Our thoughts, our inmost thoughts, have been joined by that bright inner vision, by the clairvoyance, which is our strength.

"I will be your woman, John Tabor—and together we will fight this conspiracy and destroy it. We will share other visions on Venus, and every move that the conspirators make will be known to us. We'll inform Society of their every maneuver, and we will not rest until they have been brought to justice."

I really made an effort then to untangle her arms, deciding I'd be rough about it if I had to. But she resisted my angry tugging, and clung to me with a desperate urgency.

"Do you doubt what I've told you? Do you need proof? Shall I give you proof?"

Before I could reply she pressed her lips to my throat and kissed me, so hard her teeth bruised the flesh a little. A man doesn't have to have a gram of masochism in his nature to be thrilled by that kind of "love bite"—if the woman hasn't become hateful to him. But now, more than ever, I wanted Claire to be the woman in my arms while I was making it clear to Agnes that the way I felt about the Big Brain and the monitors couldn't have been changed if I'd been offered a harem on Venus Base with from fifty to a hundred women in it. Unless, of course, they all looked like Claire and the Big

Brain agreed to blow itself up when all of the monitors were standing right under it.

"Move back against the wall. Agnes," a cold voice said.

The sound of Claire's dress was no more than a rustle, but I knew she was standing very close to us. Agnes stiffened in my arms, but before I could turn, Claire spoke again. "I'll not warn you a third time. Stand away from him and move back against the wall."

I had been right about Claire's nearness. She was standing within three feet of us and her eyes met with mine the instant I turned. She had reached down and drawn the stocking knife from Agnes' ankle. It glittered in her hand.

There are revelations so staggering that your mind goes off on a tangent. There is a moment of shock, of stunned disbelief, when you just can't get a firm grip on reality.

She was a changed Claire. Her eyes were clear and determined—and blazing with anger. "It is all true, John," Claire said. "She has opened your eyes more widely than you think. She is a very clever woman. The monitors trust her and are unwilling to believe that with her great beauty and clever tongue she will fail in her mission."

Agnes was moving reluctantly back toward the wall now, but all of my attention was centered on Claire.

She was standing very still, the knife firm in her clasp, when I whispered: "You can't be—"

"I am," Claire said.

"A real woman."

"Look at me, John. Can you doubt it? You should have known the instant you looked upon my unclothed body and told me that I was all woman."

"The most beautiful woman I ever held in my arms," I whispered. "And real!"

Yes, John.

"I was in love with you from the first moment I saw you," I said. "Did you know that?"

"I was sure of it, John. They studied your biogenetic norm data very carefully. I was the only woman they could find who was just right for you. It works both ways, John. You are just right for me."

Agnes cried, "That's a lie!"

"I think not," Claire said. "He was infatuated with you, but he loves me. He loves me enough to fight for a new life of freedom and independence on Venus."

Her eyes narrowed and she added with a candor that startled me: "Elementary sexuality can be a powerful driving force in all men and women. But it doesn't become really glorious until something more imperishable enters into it. The undying love of one man for one woman—his love for her as a *person*."

Agnes' eyes narrowed and she advanced on Claire with a cold fury in her stare. "Neither of you will live to join the conspirators," she warned. "In a few minutes you will be prisoners. You will be bound and thrown into prison. Your trial and punishment will be swift, I promise you."

I knew instantly that she could make good her threat. As an agent of Society, she would not have made a single warning move against us without complete assurance. I knew that if she struggled furiously precious time would be lost, our peril dangerously increased.

I stared at her for an instant in stunned incredulity. She was superb and resourceful, even in her desperation; Claire seemed to have sensed that resourcefulness instinctively, and was girding herself for a physical struggle that could have resulted in disaster for us both.

I leapt forward and seized Agnes about the waist. I clamped my hand over her mouth and shouted to Claire, "Get out! I'll join you down below. Hurry, darling—there's

210

no time to be lost. The Security Police will be here any minute now."

Agnes fought like a wildcat, bit, clawed and scratched. I saw Claire turn and run through the door, and I heard her footsteps descending the stairs to the street.

"You'll never get away!" Agnes' voice was choked with a despairing hatred.

"We can try," I said, almost whispering it. I tightened my grip on her waist; then with a violent wrench I freed my left arm, and sent her spinning back against the wall.

I swung about and headed for the door, I heard her cry out, but I did not turn. I leapt out into the corridor, and slammed the door shut behind me, the rusty key in my hand.

I locked the door from the outside, and headed straight down the stairs to the street. Claire was waiting for me at the foot of the stairs, standing white and motionless with one hand pressed to her throat.

"Come on," I urged, "we've got to keep moving. They'll be after us quickly enough."

We joined hands and ran together out into the street. We kept close to the buildings as we ran, our shadows lengthening grotesquely before us on the deserted pavement. We skirted walls crumbling and time-eroded, ducked in and out of refuse-littered alleyways and ran for a short distance in the open, the early morning sunlight beating unmercifully down upon us.

We were in the open when we heard the first chill far-off drone of the sirens.

I tightened my hold on Claire's hand and whispered urgently, "We won't have time to reach a subway entrance. We'll be hemmed in from all sides. We've got to hide out while the search is on."

"Where?" Claire breathed.

Ahead of us was a towering structure of crumbling gray-yellow stone. I gestured toward it and we headed for the darkly yawning entrance.

We passed together in a vast, dimly illuminated hall. On all sides of us towered incredible instruments of science crumbling into rust. We fled straight down the hall and climbed up behind a gigantic, dynamo-shaped object that vibrated hollowly as we jarred it with our bodies.

Suddenly out of the darkness a voice droned, "This is Occupational Advisory Unit 34 GH. Pick your pattern for work and living. We want you to relax fully and completely while you observe the future, as we have planned it for you. You must have mechanical aptitude of a high order or you would not have come to this Unit.

"Take your time in choosing a profession. Wander about the hall at leisure and observe the many fascinating three-dimensional cinemascopic recordings. Study steel-welding, tool-making, metal-craft designing in all their intricate ramifications. It is *your* future you are planning here. Remember—*your* future.

"The choice you make now will influence your entire future. Remember. If you make a wise choice now half of the battle will be won."

I tightened my hold on Claire's hand. "This was an ancient occupational advisory unit building," I whispered. "What you just heard was the last gasp of an expiring free society. That metaltape recording pretends to offer a choice of occupation to the poor dupes who found their way here. But even then there was an ominous undertone: *observe the future as we have planned it for you.*"

"I know," Claire whispered. "In daring now to plan our own future we may well have chosen a design for dying. But the choice had to be made; I am glad we had the courage to dare greatly."

I had learned the trick, years ago, of keeping a watertight compartment of my mind alert to danger. In one little portion of my mind a whisper in the dark, an approaching faint footstep, or dark undercurrents of hostile thoughts beating in upon me, could put me instantly on the defensive.

I suddenly knew that we were not alone in the building. I gripped Claire's wrist and drew her back into the shadows. Then I leaned cautiously forward and stared down.

There was a flickering on the stone floor far below, a faint shifting of light and shadow between the projection instruments and the cinemascopic recording screens. I realized abruptly that someone was climbing up toward us. When I strained my ears I could hear the "someone's" faint breathing.

I should have taken the initiative then and there. I should have leapt out, carried the battle to the unseen climber. I could have quickly discovered him, and his position directly beneath me would have placed him at a disadvantage. But I waited too long, and the ugly bulk of him came suddenly into view and before I could leap to my feet he covered the distance between us in a powerful but well-timed rush.

I only just ducked in time as he swung at me, both of his fists flailing. He was a Security Police officer; at his wrist an electro-sap that could have cracked my skull like a mace. It described a flashing arc with his lunge, and I could hear the deadly swish.

He went spinning past me, shifting his weight as he went to preserve his balance. He almost thudded into the wall behind me, so great and furious had been his initial onslaught. But when he pivoted about on his heels and came swinging back toward me I was ready for him.

I hit him in the stomach with a slashing right uppercut, and brought my left fist flush with his jaw with all the violence I could muster. He groaned and reeled back, and I kicked at his Achilles' tendon with the tip of my boot. The kick seemed to hurt him more than the blows; he let out a yell, ducked low, and weaved back toward me.

For a moment we traded blows, fierce and heavy; and I had to keep jabbing at him with both my fists to keep him from opening a twelve-inch gash in my chest with the electro-sap.

I floored him with one very heavy blow delivered with desperate calculation.

I'd been so busy taking care of him that it wasn't until he lay sprawled out at my feet with a little ribbon of crimson trickling from his mouth that I realized that another struggle was going on in the shadows.

I turned just in time to see Claire standing with a knife in her clasp in complete isolation from Agnes. If I'd turned a moment sooner, I might have seen Agnes emerge into view between the projection instruments, and rush straight at Claire as the Security Police officer had rushed at me. I might have seen Claire draw the knife in self-defense.

But at least I had turned in time to witness the crucial stage of the struggle, and for that I was grateful.

I was grateful in another way, for it could only mean that the Security Police had arrived to free Agnes a minute or two after we'd heard the drone of the sirens. Obviously they had trailed us to the Occupational Advisory building—the only large structure in the area—and if our departure had been delayed and they'd come after us a little faster we would have had no chance at all.

Agnes' eyes were narrowed and she was advancing on Claire with a cold fury in her stare. "Give me that knife!" she warned. "Give it to me, or I'll take it from you!"

"Just try!" Claire said.

Agnes grabbed Claire's wrist and swung her about. Before I could get between them they started struggling.

What happened then was like a scene in a dream; fantastic, wildly terrible. Agnes backed Claire against the wall and twisted her wrist cruelly. Claire resisted and fought back, but Agnes got the knife.

She let Claire break free, and then started for her. She went for Claire with the knife upraised, a killing rage in her eyes.

She went for Claire fast—too fast. Her foot slipped, and she went down face forward; and as she fell the knife twisted in her clasp.

A look of almost childlike astonishment came into her eyes.

For one awful moment she writhed about on the floor, her fingers still clasping the knife. Then a convulsive shudder shook her. Her face twisted in agony, and a dull gaze overspread her pupils. Slowly, horribly, her eyes lidded themselves and her breathing became less harsh, finally subsiding entirely. She lay still.

If you've ever seen it happen, you'll want to forget it as quickly as possible. You won't want to be tortured by it as I was, even though for one merciful instant my mind became a recording instrument solely, a gray film which registered only that quick and involuntary act of self-destruction, I felt no horror, no shock.

I was standing motionless, staring at Claire, when four men and four women emerged from the shadows. The men wore Venus Base uniforms; the women were all very beautiful, with skins like rose petals and large dark eyes that searched my face in eager curiosity. The big man who had helped us at the races stood very straight and still, staring from me to Claire with a relieved and grateful look in his eyes. He seemed even huger in his uniform. We would be indebted to him until we were too old to dream.

A tall, red-haired girl with sympathetic eyes went up to the limp form on the floor, knelt and made a hasty examination. After a moment she raised her eyes, and spoke to Claire, "Does he know?"

Claire shook her head.

"You'd better tell him," the girl advised.

Claire looked at me, her eyes compassionate. "Agnes was an android, John," she said. "Agnes was the most successful of a hundred android robots made and trained by Society in strict secrecy to spy on our activities."

The red-haired girl said, "Usually our chosen mates are not told the full truth until they are safely on Venus. But when you brought Claire here, you made a dangerous situation more complicated. Our task now is to get you both to the spaceport as quickly as possible."

She smiled. "You're as good as there already, for you'll be guarded every foot of the way by members of our organization."

I looked at Claire.

She looked at me.

I thought of Venus Base, and I thought of Claire lying in my arms, her face hidden.

Just how lucky can a man be?

THE END

www.ingramcontent.com/pod-product-compliance
Lightning Source LLC
Chambersburg PA
CBHW030308180626
46810CB00003B/981